THE RIVER BANK

THE RIVER BANK

By Sheila Tucker

ISBN: 978-0-615-27860-5

Dedication

I would like to dedicate this book to the ones who inspired me to keep going when my hope was failing.

Steve, you give me encouragement to live my dreams. I want to share my today, tomorrow and forever with you.

To Cody and April, you give me laughter. That's all the medicine I ever need.

To all my family, friends, and co-workers who patiently waited for the ending, thank you.

Foreword

This is a work of fiction. Names, characters, places, and incidents either are the product of the author's imagination or are used fictitiously, and any resemblance to actual persons, living or dead, business establishments, events, or locales is entirely coincidental.

Contents

Chapter 1

It was a sunny day on the banks of the Ouachita River. The temperature was 92 but the humidity pulled on you like a two-year-old in a candy store. Canoes floated swiftly by with laughing couples enjoying the day, their shoulders as red as the clay dirt on the shore. It was just another Sunday afternoon in Arkansas. That was all about to change for two teenage boys out for some fun.

Sean Fisher and Bobby Timmons were juniors at Magnet Cove High School. Best friends since first grade, you wouldn't find one without the other. Some laughingly called them "The Twins" even though they looked as different as beans and potatoes. Bobby was a blond headed, blue eyed girls dream, while Sean was a true carrot top with smiling green eyes. Their classmates would say they were the class clowns. Their teachers would say they needed to work on their grades. The principal would say they were trouble makers. Any way you looked at it, the two friends had nothing more in mind that day than a little voyeurism.

It was common knowledge where all the girls went to skinny dip in the bend of the river. There, where the old oak trees hang low over the banks of the water, girls of all ages used the privacy provided to swim in nothing more than God gave them. Of course they knew the boys liked to try to sneak in to get a free peep show, so one girl would always be posted as a lookout. Most boys never got within fifty feet of the clothes strewn bank before a warning would go out. But on this day, the warning never came.

Kimberly Short was designated whistle blower on this Sunday. Kim was sixteen, the youngest in the group gathered for a swim. She was slim with short brown hair and a smile that made all the boys wonder how close they could get to those lips. For her, high school was one step further in a career in journalism. With her column in the school paper and her pages in the yearbook, her love of writing showed in every pencil stroke. Mrs. Briggs, the journalism teacher, would have loved to take the credit for her talented young pupil, but even she knew Kim had a natural talent for writing. Kim was well on her way to her dream scholarship at St. Johns University in New York with a 4.0 grade point average. She was always joking that all the best writers are from New York.

Kim would never get to New York. For on the river that day with the girls, an evil waited to envelope them. As the water gurgled along the rocky undertow, girls laughing at the feel of grit between their toes, death waited behind the guard of the trees. Some of those swimming that day would later recall how a sudden chill had settled over them and drove them from the water searching for warmth. They would state how after getting dressed, they called for Kim with the all clear signal. She never answered that call. When the group went into the woods to search for her, all laughter had ceased and an unease had begun to grow. As the girls stepped into the clearing about thirty yards from the shore, they stumbled across a gruesome scene. Kim was lying face down in a pool of blood, with two teenage boys nearby, one kneeling beside the body. As chaos reigned, one girl managed to dial 9-1-1 on her cell phone. Other girls ran from the scene; a few were frozen with fear, and a couple lost what little lunch they had eaten. The first responders to the sight immediately called for more backup. It would take the combined efforts of several law enforcement agencies to get control of the scene. But the truth would be a long time in coming.

What happened that day, on the banks of the river, would change the lives of everyone in that small town. For some, life would be broken, never to return to the peaceful existence of day to day life. Opinions would divide a community and controversy would settle in. Rumors would fly and conversations in the coffee shops would center on what actually happened that day. When the facts started to surface, no one could have guessed where the truth would lead. From innocence lost to a cold blooded killer in disguise, only the river bank could give the answers everyone was looking for.

Chapter 2

S ergeant Malone was tired. Six hours straight of digging
through mud and leaves, trying hard to avoid the blood, had
him wishing for a cold beer and a warm bed. This was the worst
part; the iron smell of the blood, the eyes staring at nothing, the
knowing that someone, somewhere was crying wishing for a
loved one to come home. After thirty years as a police officer,
you would think he'd get used to it. Oh, the blood didn't bother
him much, what with police work and Vietnam, he'd seen a lot of
senseless killing in his time. Hell, he'd caused some of it. But
something about this crime scene bothered Malone-a lot.

Maybe it was the age of the victim. Maybe it was the age
of the suspects. He couldn't quite put his finger on it, yet some
little something didn't feel right. It made his thigh hurt. And
when Malone's thigh hurt, every muscle, every joint, every
nerve, stood up and listened. That thigh had been talking to
Malone ever since he had gotten home from Vietnam, with a
medal for bravery and a piece of shrapnel buried in his leg. And
right now, all he could hear it say was, something ain't right.
What struck him the most is what he didn't hear.

What Malone wasn't hearing was why. Why Kim? Why these boys? It just didn't make any sense. With every crime, save for the criminally insane, there was a motive. Sex, drugs, money, vengeance, any of these were answers to that age old question of why. But this crime scene didn't fit any of those. There was no initial sign of a sexual assault, drugs were out of the equation, and Malone was pretty sure there hadn't been any money stashed in her bathing suit. So that left vengeance. The only problem with that was everyone liked Kim. Malone couldn't find a single person that had a grudge against her. Not one. And these boys just brought up more questions. Sure the boys had gotten into some trouble a few times but nothing like this. The only record they had was from Halloween last year when they rolled the principal's house. Mr. Brady just happened to be having a sleepless night and caught them in the act. Parents were called, the boys had some cleaning up to do, and a misdemeanor criminal mischief charge was all that came from that. These boys just weren't the type to do this. So what did Malone's evidence say?

The truth was, the evidence in this case wasn't saying a whole lot yet. Between nine teenage girls, three first responders, and a slew of police officers, detectives, and one coroner, the evidence had pretty much been trampled. What Malone could salvage told of a violent stabbing death, probably with a serrated edged hunting knife. The coroner estimated seven distinct stab wounds to the torso. It was definitely overkill. Two of the wounds would have punctured the heart and one lung. Kim wasn't going anywhere after those. The killer had not left behind the murder weapon. No, that probably would have been too easy. Blood evidence was abundant with spatter on trees, bushes, and also on two teenage boys. But why?

Both boys told the same story; a day of spying on naked girls turned into a nightmare. Bobby said he was the first to discover the body. He was in the lead trying to find a trail the girls wouldn't hear or see them coming from. When he stumbled onto the scene, his first reaction was to help. He tried to roll her over but Sean stopped him. Sean didn't want any part of this. Blood made him sick anyway and he wanted to get as far away as possible. As Sean backed away, the rest of the girls broke through the brush and all hell broke loose. Bobby had blood on his hands, knees, and shoes. Sean had managed to only get blood on his hands and the bottom of his shoes. He said the only way he had gotten it on his hands was when he grabbed Bobby to keep him from turning Kim over. Malone was hoping that mixed in with all that blood would be a little piece of the killer waiting to speak out. Stabbing was messy work and the perps usually ended up with a few cuts themselves. DNA was a wonderful tool that Malone thanked God for every time he had a bloody crime scene. He could only wait and see what fate had in store for him today.

For now, it would be a waiting game for the coroner to do his part. Once Malone had an autopsy report, he could begin to piece together what happened. He was going home to a hot shower, some leftover pizza from last night, and then to bed. Maybe something would click while he was sleeping. Who knew what would come to him in his dreams. Tomorrow he could start fresh and get down to digging up the truth.

Meanwhile, a couple of boys were wishing for their homes but instead were looking at four walls with a door they weren't allowed to use

....

Sitting in interrogation, Bobby could almost hear his mom in the kitchen cooking supper. God how he wished he was there right now. But then again, he knew his mom wasn't in her kitchen, she was sitting outside talking to the detectives. He had only seen a glimpse of her as she went by the door when the last detective went out. He had hated to see the fear on her face and the trace of tears he saw in her eyes. If he was up to admitting things, the first thing would be that her eyes weren't the only ones with tears in them. He was scared, more than he had ever been in his life. And that was saying a lot when you consider what he went through last summer. But enough of that. He had to find a way to convince these cops that he didn't kill that girl. Just thinking about her made his skin wrinkle up with goose bumps. She was a beautiful girl, Kim, he thought they'd said, but those eyes. He knew he would never forget those eyes as long as he lived. He'd be seeing those in dreams for years to come. If he had years to live. Why, oh why, did he have to touch her. Instinct he guessed. Sean had been right when he grabbed him and said, "Don't!". Just one little word but what meaning it could have had.

Bobby's head hurt what with all the questions, accusations, and that one detective, what was his name? Oh, yeah, Cooper. He had a way of tapping that damn pen on the desk. It made Bobby want to snatch it away and fling it as far away from them as possible. But that probably wouldn't be a good idea. He looked guilty enough as it was. How could they even think for a minute that he was capable of something like that? If they only knew him then he wouldn't be sitting here right now. He'd be home eating mom's meatloaf with mashed potatoes and green beans. His little sister, Jamie, would be bugging him to play Barbie dolls with her. How many times did he have to tell her, boys don't play with dolls? He must be more tired than he thought if he was thinking about Barbies.

What was happening to Sean? Was Sean as screwed up as he was? When could they go home? He knew that when he and Sean rolled Mr. Brady's house, all it took was their parents signing some papers and a court date and they were free to go home. Not too free, though. They both spent their weekends doing chores around the house and cleaning up the toilet paper at Mr. Brady's for a few months. His mom didn't say a whole lot. But he could tell he had disappointed her and that hurt worse than any punishment she could have dished out. He hoped she knew he could never have done this. Not in a million years. Where were the detectives? When was his mom coming in to get him? His head was exploding with questions but no one to answer them. Those stupid tears were starting up again. He thought, please, God, don't let anyone see me like this.

In another room, Sean was fighting back.

....

Sean was mad; madder than he had ever been in his life. He was used to people saying he had a temper, after all he did have red hair. But this was more than he was willing to deal with. Words he never thought he would say to anyone were coming from his lips. The problem was, saying them didn't make things any better. That girl was still dead and he still had her blood on his hands. He sure would like to go back in time and do things a little different. He sure as hell wouldn't grab Bobby's hands again. Fact is, he would probably stay in bed all day if he could do it all over again. Wishes only come true in fairy tales, though, and a fairy godmother wasn't popping up in the interrogation room.

Cooper was talking again. "Boy, we're just trying to help you. You know you'll feel better when you come clean and tell us what happened. Hell, Bobby's probably over there right now telling them all about how you planned all this. If you want us to know the real truth you'd better speak up now."

"I've told you the truth but you won't listen. If Bobby says I planned this it's because ya'll made him say it. I'm not saying what isn't true. I never saw that girl before today when we about stepped on her. She was already dead. There wasn't a thing in the world we could do for her. I'm sorry she's dead but I didn't do it!"

"So Bobby did it then? Is that-"

"Where the hell you been in the last two minutes? I just got through telling you we come up on her after she was dead. How the hell is Bobby going to kill her when he was with me the whole time?"

Deputy Shankles stepped in, "Sean, calm down. We can't get to the bottom of this if you get so uptight Cooper here wants to stomp on you. Let's go back to the beginning again. You and Bobby only wanted to get a look at the girls swimming naked, right?"

"That's what I told you an hour ago and that's what I'm saying now. Everybody knows that's the place the girls always skinny dip. Nobody's been able to sneak up on them yet though, and we thought for sure we had found the perfect trail. All we wanted was to be the first to make it up close without getting caught."

"So you'd never seen this girl before today?"

"No. She's not from Magnet Cove. I don't think I've seen her around or I probably would have remembered her."

"Did you see anyone else on the trail or remember hearing anything?"

"No. We were concentrating on being as quiet as possible. If we weren't hearing anything, we figured neither were the girls."

Cooper started tapping his pen again. "You want to know what I think, Shankles? I think this here boy couldn't keep his hands to himself. He and his little buddy next door went for a little peep show and what they got was a real live girl just sitting there all pretty waiting on 'em. They decided to take it just a little bit further than looking but that girl was feisty and wouldn't give it up. So they had to shut her up. Ain't that what happened boy?"

This was the last straw. Sean jumped up, kicked his chair across the room shouting, "Shut the hell up! You don't know what you're talking about! I never touched that girl!"

In a flash Cooper had him pinned down to the table with an elbow in his neck.

"What do you think, Shankles? Think I ought to break his scrawny neck?"

"Let him go, Cooper. You know the Chief said even one more little hint of misbehaving and you would be back to filing papers again. He's going to behave, aren't you Sean?"

Cooper let go and Sean stood up and flexed his neck. If hate could cut across a room, Cooper would be the one needing an autopsy.

Sean asked, "Where's my parents? I want to talk to Mom and Dad. I don't know the law that much but I think I can at least talk to them."

"They're already here but they are talking to some other detectives right now. Would you like something to drink?" Detective Shankles needed to see what was going on outside and see if any new information was available yet.

"Sure. You got a soda? I don't care what kind. And would you see if my parents are coming to talk to me soon?"

Cooper snorted and said something to the effect of they'd be better off cutting their losses, slamming the door as he left. Doug Shankles looked back catching a glimpse of fear on Sean's face. If Doug was a betting man, he'd lay pretty good odds that a killer was on the loose tonight because eyes like that don't lie. Those were the eyes of a child waking from a nightmare, begging to be held and told there were no monsters under the bed. The problem was, Doug wasn't so sure there weren't.

Chapter 3

L inda Timmons picked up the wadded tissue, twisting it as if by doing so all the tears she had cried would disappear. A single mother, she was used to crisis and having to deal with it all on her own. Her husband had left four years ago, leaving her with two children, a mountain of debt, and a bruised ego. He had told her quite plainly that living with her had made him miserable so he was off to find a better life with a woman who could make him happy just by looking at her. She had managed to survive by looking in the face of her kids knowing they were dependent on her to keep the family going. With no work experience to speak of, Linda had enrolled at the local college on a PELL grant seeking a degree in cosmetology. She worked the evening shift at Wal-Mart to bring in a little money. It was rough for a while but the kids had held up well, staying with a friend while Linda was working. Once she graduated, she managed to talk her way into Barb's Beauty Shop as a hairstylist. It took a while for her to prove herself but now she had a pretty good clientele built up. She had quit Wal-Mart as soon as her hair styling had taken off so she could be home with Bobby and Jamie in the evenings. Sometimes she couldn't imagine how she would have made it without her kids and yet, sometimes, she wondered how she managed not to strangle the both of them. Oh she knew they were good kids, she had seen her fair share of rotten ones, but she just needed a break ever now and then.

Thinking of that now, sitting at a desk in front of a detective, she prayed that her break wouldn't come in the form of her son going to jail. Bobby wouldn't have done what they said he did. She knew that with all her motherly intuition and ever fiber of her heart and soul. If he had blood on his hands it was because he was trying to help. Bobby had a soft spot for injured things, always bringing home small animals for her to nurse back to health. If she had let him have his way, their whole house would be filled with strays. Why couldn't these officers see that? Did they even care?

"Mrs. Timmons, I know this is hard on you to understand, but I can't just ignore the fact that a young girl is dead and your son was found next to her with blood on his hands."

Lieutenant Mike Darby could tell this was a lot more than she could take in right now. Having to tell a parent their child was in this much trouble wasn't easy. Then again, having to talk to Kimberly Short's parents had been even harder. The Chaplain had been a godsend to the department for just such an occasion.

"I really feel the best thing for you to do is to get a good attorney for Bobby."

"Lieutenant, I live on a small income and with no help from anyone when it comes to money. The only attorney I know is my divorce attorney and even he had to let me pay him out. If you know a good attorney that will work with me, I'd appreciate it. All I want now is to take my son home. I can sign whatever papers you want me to saying I'll be responsible for him. He'll stay with me every minute of the day if I have to chain him to my leg."

"It's not that simple. Murder is not something we can just let go on a signature bond. He'll have to go before the juvenile court judge to enter a plea and then the judge can set bail. The court can appoint Bobby an attorney and he'll be able to guide you through the process."

"Can I at least talk to Bobby? He must be scared out of his mind right now."

"I can let you see him for a few minutes but then he'll have to go to juvenile detention for tonight. I'll talk to the court in the morning to set up a hearing and call you as soon as I know something. Here's my card. This is my cell number and my home number, call me anytime if I can be of help. I want this cleared up just as much as you do."

"Thank you so much for your time and trouble. I swear to you, my Bobby didn't do this. You're looking in the wrong direction. Whoever killed that young girl is still out there."

"Believe me ma'am, we are investigating all possible leads at this point. We have our best detectives working on this and overtime is no object."

As they walked to the door, Doug Shankles was walking by with a soda in his hand. Lieutenant Darby stopped him.

"Doug, can you take Mrs. Timmons to see her son? I've told her she can talk to him for a few minutes. When she's done, come into my office."

"Sure thing, sir. Let me drop off this drink for the other suspect."

Linda waited while Doug took the can to Sean. She wondered how he was doing and if Richard and Candy were in with him. They must be as blown away by all this as she was. She sent a silent prayer up for all of them. They all needed as much help as they could get.

Deputy Shankles reappeared and with a small smile led her to a room on the left. As the door opened, Linda broke down. Bobby jumped up as soon as she came in and both embraced, tears mingling with tears. For a moment neither spoke, choosing instead to cling to each other in silent communication. Finally, with a sniffle, Bobby let go of his death grip on his mom and stepped back.

"I'm so sorry Mom. I didn't do it, I swear I didn't. But they don't believe me."

Linda kept a firm grip on his hands, squeezing them slightly.

"I know you didn't, sweetie, I know. It's going to be alright. We're going to get you an attorney and everything will be ok. You'll see. He'll have you out in no time and we will be able to sort everything out, ok?

You listen to me, I love you and nothing is going to change that. You be honest with them, tell them the truth and everything will work out fine."

"I am telling the truth. I know we shouldn't have even been there but we didn't hurt anybody. I thought she was just hurt and I was going to help her. Did they say when I could go home?"

"No. A judge will have to set bail before you can come home. I'm going to get as much money as we need, don't worry. You'll be home by tomorrow."

"By tomorrow? Where will I go tonight?"

"You'll go to a juvenile detention home tonight."

"But I didn't do anything wrong, Mom. Can't you sign for me to go home now?"

"No, it doesn't work that way this time. But I will get you out as soon as possible. You'll be ok I promise. Look at me Bobby. Promise me you'll take care of yourself until I come to get you."

Linda looked her son in the eye, saw the fear, and it was all she could do not to grab him and run. Never in her life as a mother had she felt this helpless. It was a feeling she didn't want to ever repeat. Her heart was breaking and with her hands cupping his face, she silently vowed to move heaven and earth to never see that look in his eyes again. She swiftly gave him a kiss on the cheek, the salty taste of tears a testimony to the agony Bobby was going through.

Bobby felt his mothers hands leave his face and he closed his eyes. He didn't want to watch her walk away, knowing that when she did, he was on his own. He also didn't want her to see him crying anymore, not wanting to cause her any more pain. In that moment, Bobby's youth disappeared and a maturity surfaced. An instinctive need to protect her made him open his eyes. With a watery smile he glanced once more at his mother. With a whispered "I love you" he watched her walk through the door.

....

Richard and Candy Fisher were at that moment wondering how on earth Sean could have gotten himself into this mess. After trying for eight years to have a child, the couple had given up all hopes and decided to adopt. The adoption process was a long one but Candy never wavered. She wanted to hold a baby in her arms, one she wouldn't have to give back to another woman when the baby cried for a bottle. Richard loved his wife dearly and would have done anything to wipe away the sadness he saw in her eyes every time she watched a new mother nursing her baby. He never questioned her judgment, either, when she chose the little redheaded boy out of all the pictures they were shown. Candy said he needed her, she could tell by his eyes.

After the adoption was final, the Fishers brought Sean home for the first time on Valentines Day. Candy thought it was a sign from God for them to finally have their child on a day set aside for love. And love him she did. Sean never wanted for anything. Richard would sometimes tease her that she knew when Sean was going to cry before the baby did. Neither would call Sean spoiled even though his temper would flair up occasionally. He was a sweet natured child always laughing and joking around. He had plenty of friends growing up but never one as close as Bobby.

Candy knew Linda from the church ladies group and it only seemed natural for the boys to become friends. Candy helped out as much as possible when Linda's husband left. Linda walked around in a daze for a while, reminding Candy of a deer looking down the barrel of a gun. Once she got on her feet, though, Linda never looked back. Self pity didn't put food on the table or pay the electric bill. The two ladies shared a love for the church, a love for sappy movies, and a love born of motherhood.

Richard was a hard worker, working rotating shifts at the local cable mill. He was a loving father and husband who shared this love with only one other thing: deer hunting. If passion had a name, for him it would be deer season. Every year on the first day of October, Richard was in the deer stand with a quiver on his right side and his Browning compound bow on his left. Hunting was a sport but it was also a get away for Richard. When he was hunting, he forgot about the problems at work, the union dues, and the worry about retirement. It was nature at it's greatest as he saw it. He had a natural sense of direction that enabled him to travel into unfamiliar woods without losing his way. He was also a quiet man and the peace of the woods made him a firm believer that heaven must have trees. Killing a deer was only part of the draw Richard felt for hunting. A kill meant meat in the freezer but hunting also gave him a sense of accomplishment. It was the one thing he was really good at.

Thinking back now to the first time he had taken Sean hunting with him, Richard knew without a doubt, this was all wrong. They had it all wrong. That first deer hunt, Sean managed to kill a young doe with a new rifle Richard had bought him. As Richard, ecstatic that his son was carrying on in his footsteps, brought Sean up to the deer, something unexpected happened. The sight of the doe lying motionless, eyes starting to glaze, did not bring Sean joy. Instead, he fell to his knees, vomiting, begging Richard to take him home. Later, when Sean finally consented to talk about it, the truth was harsh for Richard. Sean hated blood. He hated the smell of it, the look of it, and the knowledge that he had caused it bothered him. Although Richard was disappointed, he agreed that Sean would not go hunting again.

Richard had learned to accept this about Sean focusing instead on other things the two could do together. On Saturdays, if the weather was nice and Richard wasn't working graveyard that week, four wheelers were loaded into the pickup for a quick trip to the trails. Sean seemed to enjoy their rides and this way Richard got a chance to share a little of his passion with Sean. They rarely talked when they were out there, choosing to enjoy the scenery and the bonding moments.

As Richard and Candy sat waiting to see Sean, both were lost in thoughts of their son and how to get him home. Several detectives walked by but none stopped to let them know what was going on. One detective came out of a room across from where they were sitting, giving them a sneering look before walking away. Candy reached for Richard's hand, hers cold and shaking from fear. Richard absently rubbed her hand with his callused ones, noticing suddenly how small she seemed.

When the door opened again, Candy sprang up not wanting to waste another minute.

"Please, can you tell me where my son is? His name is Sean Fisher and there has been some big mistake."

Doug looked at the petite woman, saw the unmistakable look of fear and never doubted the sincerity of it. If he could do nothing else today, he wanted to take away that look, the same one he had seen just moments ago.

"Ma'am, let me take you to the chief. He can answer your questions for you. It's right this way."

"Thank you so much. We've been waiting for a while but no one has told us anything other than what the phone call said."

They followed Doug down the hall past several doors before stopping in front of a large office door with "Chief Deputy" engraved on a silver star hanging on the door. Doug knocked twice before opening the door.

"Chief, the Fishers are here. Shall I bring them in?"

Chief Deputy Olen Brown stood up as Richard and Candy came in. Reaching across the desk scattered with folders, photos, and pens, he offered his hand to Richard.

"I'm Chief Deputy Olen Brown. I talked to you on the phone earlier."

"Yes sir. I'm Richard and this is my wife Candy. We are still unsure just what is going on. You think my son killed a girl?"

Candy spoke up immediately, "That's impossible! My Sean wouldn't hurt a fly much less kill a girl."

"Ma'am, as much as I would like to believe you, the evidence is stating otherwise. Sean and another boy, Bobby Timmons, were both found at the crime scene, beside the body, both with blood on them."

"Sir, no disrespect intended, but did the boys say they killed this girl?" Richard needed to hear the answer to this.

"No, sir, they didn't. Both boys are adamantly denying it. But we have to go by evidence found at the scene and so far all the evidence points to Sean and Bobby. Both boys are still being questioned by my detectives. We will have to hold them until a judge decides what to do with them."

"You mean we can't take Sean home?" Candy asked.

"No ma'am, not tonight. You can speak to him only for a few minutes but then we will have to transfer him to juvenile detention. Tomorrow, Judge Marshall will be in and you can see about bail then."

"Richard, they are taking my baby to jail. Can't you do something?"

"Candy, let's go talk to Sean ok? Don't worry about jail right now. I want to talk to Sean."

Olen picked up the phone and dialed quickly.

"Cooper, come to my office now please."

After a moment, during which the silence grew intense, the door opened and the same deputy who had given Candy the sneer came in. Olen asked him to take the couple to see Sean. While walking to the interrogation room, Candy shivered as she neared Cooper. She had never personally believed in a person who made your hair stand on end, but now she knew exactly what they meant by that. This man is not on our side, Candy thought. He doesn't care if Sean is innocent or not.

Once Cooper opened the door, all thoughts of him left Candy's mind. Sean was sitting in a hard metal chair with his head down on the table in front of him. His red hair was sticking up in places telling Candy he had been running his fingers through it just like he always did when he's upset. Sean was dozing and didn't notice at first that anyone had come in.

Cooper banged the table with his hand startling everyone and causing Sean to jump.

"Wake up sleeping beauty, your folks are here."

"Mom, Dad, finally."

Candy rushed over to Sean gripping him in a hug. Her head only reached his shoulder yet Sean lovingly let her hold him. Richard came up beside him, grabbing his shoulders.

"How are you son?"

"I'm ok I guess. I'm tired and ready to go home, though."

"You ain't going nowhere yet, boy. They're only here to talk to you. You get to spend the night with us."

Richard shot a look of anger at Cooper.

"Could you please leave us alone to talk to our son?"

"Sure thing. But I'll be right outside so don't get any funny ideas. The Chief said a couple of minutes so I'll be back soon."

Sean watched him go dreading his return.

"Tell us what happened Sean. We only got a few details from the Chief before we came." Richard didn't want to waste any time, knowing that Cooper would keep his word.

"Dad, me and Bobby went to the river just to mess around. You know we've been talking about how the right person could sneak up on those girls without them even knowing it. Well, we found the trail we had been looking for and we were close to the river when we found her. I don't know who she was but Bobby pushed through a patch of brush and I about stepped on him when I came out. She was just laying there, blood everywhere, not moving. Bobby had already reached down to turn her over when I grabbed him and told him not to. The smell was already starting to get to me when all of a sudden all these girls come out ahead of us. They all started screaming at once, I saw one girl pass out, a couple threw up, and the next thing I know, the cops are there. I thought they were going to call an ambulance but they didn't. It all happened so fast I couldn't tell you what any of the cops said but I know we were thrown down and handcuffed quick enough. We tried to tell them we didn't do it but they wouldn't listen. Once we got here, they split us up. I haven't seen Bobby since. They keep asking me the same questions over and over again, like they don't want to hear what really happened."

The door opened and all three looked up expecting to see Cooper back again, but Deputy Shankles came in with a soda in his hand.

"Here you go Sean. Hope you like Coke alright."

"That's great, thanks."

Richard reached out his hand,

"Thank you for your kindness. Most of them here believe the worst of my son but I appreciate your professionalism."

Doug was touched. He couldn't imagine what he would be feeling if it was one of his kids in here. He hoped Sean was telling the truth. Doug was a firm believer in the system and if these boys were lying the system would deal with them. Until then, he would do what he could to make it easier on everyone.

"Sean, we're going to get you out as soon as we can. Your father and I know you didn't do this. Wait and see, they'll find the real killer and you and Bobby will be back to your old antics in no time."

"I hope so Mom. I'm sorry I got you both into this. I know I haven't been the greatest kid you could have but I promise I'll do better. I'll straighten up I swear."

"Don't you dare even think we're mad at you. We're just worried is all. We love you no matter what."

Cooper came in with a smile, telling them it was time to go. Richard looked into his son's eyes, remembering his wife's certainty that he needed her, and felt not for the first time, her uncanny ways of seeing things no one else could see.

....

Unknown to all those inside the sheriff's office that evening, outside the hounds had started to gather.

Chapter 4

The first media to get the news of the murder was the local paper, "The Daily Sentinel." The editor in chief sent his best reporter to cover the breaking story. He wanted front page coverage by tomorrow telling who, what, when, why, and how. Carol Watkins arrived at the sheriff's office at 9:45 p.m., camera and tape recorder ready. She was politely told to go away. The sheriff would issue statements to all media as soon as the facts became available.

Carol walked slowly outside, hoping to get a glimpse of someone suspicious or a conversation she could eavesdrop on. She was on the phone to the editor when the Channel 6 news crew arrived in a whirl of activity unloading cameras, microphones, lights, and wiring. Apparently, one of the newscasters for Channel 6 has a sister who lives in Malvern who heard the news of the murder on her police scanner. After the police ordered the net secured, the sister couldn't get any more information. She got on the phone to Channel 6 and in no time a crew was in route. Channel 9 got a whiff of the story from the Channel 6 crew so they loaded up and weren't far behind.

The sheriff was not happy. It was bad enough that a 16 year old girl had been killed in his town and now he had the media sniffing around like bloodhounds on the scent of an escaped convict. He knew he would have to give them something or rumors would take over and then there would be no telling what got put on the morning news.

Sheriff Jeremy Bailey wasn't much of a talker. He preferred to listen instead. To his way of thinking, you learned more that way. He also knew how to bullshit his way out of giving up information he didn't want to give. In this case, he was going to have to throw the dogs a bone.

As the Sheriff stepped outside, conversations came to a halt. The soft spoken man on the steps already had his audiences' full attention. He began by thanking them for their patience. He realized it was late and everyone would rather be at home in their beds, so he would make it brief. Hot Spring County deputies had been called to the scene of a possible homicide at approximately 1:45 p.m. that afternoon. Once on the scene deputies discovered the body of a young female. Witnesses were being interviewed and two suspects were being questioned in the case. Pending autopsy reports and notification of family, no names or other information could be given at this time.

He finished by thanking them for coming out and asked that the media please respect the family of the victim by letting the Sheriff's Office complete it's investigation quietly.

As soon as he finished speaking, reporters all spoke at once asking questions. How old was the victim? Were the suspects admitting to the crime? What was the cause of death? Could the citizens rest easy knowing that the police had the killer behind bars? Question after question was fired in rapid succession giving the Sheriff no time to respond and a migraine to boot. He politely stated that he had no further information at this time before walking back inside, shutting out the crowd and the questioning. Sighing, he wondered not for the first time why he chose police work as a career. His mama tried to tell him to be a fireman and days like today had him wishing he had listened to her.

....

Malvern is a small community of about ten thousand. If you're not related to someone, chances are you went to school with them or someone in their family. When word got out that one of their girls had been murdered, the whole town wanted vengeance; not justice, not closure, just pure, old school vengeance. It didn't take long for everyone to find out who the victim was and who the suspects were. Sheriff Bailey could have saved himself a headache and just spilled his guts. Since he didn't, rumors soon turned into the truth as far as the town could figure. Before Monday afternoon, Kim had been raped, strangled, duct taped, and shot. No one in the community knew the real truth so they just made it up.

The media didn't help matters. Stubbornly refusing to leave the front lawn of the Sheriff's office, news crews battled to be the first to air new information about the murder. Every person who came out of the doors that day was mobbed by reporters asking how they were related to the case. One poor man was practically assaulted as he went in to pay a traffic ticket. He had a hard time convincing the news crew that he wasn't the father of the victim or the suspects.

When Sergeant Malone showed up at the office that morning, reporters scrambled to get a statement from him. One fierce gaze from the 6'2", 210 pound man was enough to send all but the most daring retreating into the shade. Very descriptively, he told them all where they could put their microphones. He was here to solve a crime and the sooner they moved, the sooner he could do that. Malone was not known for his diplomacy. His philosophy was life was hard so in order to beat it, you had to be harder.

Once inside, Malone went to Olen Brown's office. Already gathered inside the crowded office with the Chief, were

Lieutenant Darby, Doug Shankles, and Mark Cooper. Malone squeezed in catching the tail end of a conversation.

"I still think the little punks did it. Knife or no knife, they're the only ones who had the chance. They both said they were creeping in there so the girls couldn't hear 'em coming. I think they chunked the knife when they realized they were going to get caught."

"Cooper, if they did it, why'd they stick around? They would have had an opportunity to run before we showed up." Doug still wasn't sure they had the right person or persons responsible.

"Malone, what did you find out there yesterday?" Olen asked.

"Not a whole lot. There were foot prints everywhere but we'll probably never be able to tell who's is who. I didn't find a knife so if one of the boys threw it, he's got a pretty good arm. Blood evidence was abundant but the lab will have to sort out if any of it didn't belong to the victim. I'm hoping the killer cut himself in the process. Did either of the boy's have cuts on their hands?"

"Both had scratches but nothing major. Those could have come from the briars they went through to get in there. We scraped their nails to check for skin from the body. Neither one had an excess of blood on them. If they did it, they somehow managed to stay pretty clean. I guess we'll have to wait and see what the lab has for us," Doug said.

Lieutenant Darby spoke up, "I need to go see the prosecutor this morning. With as little evidence as we have, we're going to have a hard time holding those boys much longer. Malone, are you going back out there? We need to find that knife."

"Yeah, I'm heading out in a few minutes. I was hoping ya'll might have something else for me to go on."

Just then the phone rang. Olen answered.

"Chief Deputy Olen Brown how may I help you? Yes sir, what do you have for me?"

A short pause later, "Speak English doc, I'm a simple man."

"Yeah we kind of figured that. What else?" Another pause.

"You're kidding, right? Great, this is just great. Anything else you want to throw on me? Alright, send it all over and thanks."

The Chief hung up slowly trying to digest what he had just learned.

"What is it, Chief?" Malone asked.

"That was the coroner. Official cause of death was as we already knew, homicide by exsanguinating hemorrhage. She bled out basically. She was stabbed 7 times, her heart was punctured as well as one lung. No sign of sexual assault but he sent off a rape kit just in case. But now we have another issue."

Within ten minutes, everyone had their roles set out for them. Mike went to talk to the Shorts which left Doug Shankles going to the Prosecuting Attorney's office, Cooper went to bring Sean and Bobby back to the station for more questioning, and Malone was told to find the murder weapon even if he had to go swimming to get it. After everyone was gone, Olen sat back in his chair thinking about his own daughter in college. He had seen a lot of violence in his career, things he wished he hadn't, but he tried to never take it home with him. Now, he couldn't help but think that this could have been his daughter and wondered how he would handle having her taken from him forever. He didn't envy Mike Darby his task.

．．

Jim and Rebecca Short were still in shock. Neighbors came over to provide sympathy, food, and to complain about the evil in the world today. Reverend Peterson from the Short's church came by to express his sorrow. Anyone close enough to the Reverend that day got an ear full about the wages of sin and the fires of hell. Some thought he went a little too far, and others agreed whole heartedly. Kim's parents just wanted everyone to go away so they could grieve the loss of their beautiful little girl.

Before he left, Reverend Peterson told the Shorts to pray for Kim's soul just as he would be praying for her. God would take care of her, he assured them. Still numb, they thanked him for his concern and told him they would be contacting him soon about funeral arrangements. Kim's aunt Lisa took control of the situation as soon as she came in. One look at her sister and brother-in-law told her they weren't capable of dealing with anything right now. Shooing everyone away with a thank-you and promise-to-call-if-we-need-you, Lisa managed to get some breathing room for the grieving couple.

Lisa was on the phone with the funeral home when Lieutenant Darby and the Chaplain came by. Jim and Rebecca sat down on the couch before asking Mike if he had any news about who killed Kim. Mike wasn't looking forward to the conversation he knew was coming.

"We are still in the process of interviewing the two boys found at the scene. Both boys are saying that Kim was already dead when they found her. We haven't been able to locate the knife at this time although our detectives are still searching the area. We're not giving up. We will solve this."

"Lieutenant, do you think these boys did this to my Kim?" Rebecca asked.

"Ma'am, I couldn't say one way or another just yet. I'm not ruling anything out but I'm also not ready to let them go just because they say they didn't do it. If they did, the evidence will prove it. I need to share some information with you that we received this morning. The coroner's report came in with his findings. He found seven distinct stab wounds to Kim's chest. Three of those would have been fatal blows. The other four were superficial wounds. Kim had a few defensive wounds on her hands. There was no initial sign of a sexual assault. Her death was ruled a homicide by stabbing. The coroner did find one issue that I need to discuss with you. I really don't know an easy way to say this but Kim was pregnant, about 12 weeks along."

Rebecca started sobbing. Jim was too stunned to speak. Lisa rushed over to hold Rebecca asking,

"Is he sure?"

"Yes ma'am. I'm sorry to be the one to tell you all. I take it that Kim hadn't told you?"

Jim finally spoke up, "No, she never said a word. She didn't even have a boyfriend that we knew about."

"She would have told me about a baby. Kim was a good girl, she never got into trouble, she was always in her room writing for either the paper or the yearbook. She didn't go out much and when she did it was with the girls. She would have told me, wouldn't she?" Rebecca looked at Jim, pleading with him to make sense of it all. Jim couldn't.

"Did she have a best friend that she might have confided in? Girls will sometimes tell their best friends things they wouldn't tell their parents."

"Her best friend was Kelly. She moved away about six months ago, though. Her father got transferred with the Army. They stayed in touch through letters. I guess I could try to find her address. We'll have to let her know about Kim anyway. There's so much I need to do." Rebecca started to cry again.

Lisa spoke up. "Did Kim keep a diary, Becka? She might have written something in it that would help."

"She did keep one but I don't know where. To be honest I never felt the need to look for it. She was such a good kid that I trusted her. I never would have intruded on her privacy like that. I'll go see if I can find it."

Rebecca and Lisa went to look for the diary. Jim was still sitting stoically looking down at his hands. In the last 24 hours, he had found out his daughter had been brutally murdered and that she had been pregnant and hadn't told them. His world was spinning with questions, the foremost being did they really know Kim as well as they had thought?

Mike sat for a minute, knowing that Jim was caught up in his own thoughts. Finally he spoke again quietly.

"I know all of this is a shock and I want to get to the bottom of this as much as you do. We need to find out who the father of Kim's child was and if he knew about the baby. If you can think of anyone we might could talk to please let us know."

"I really can't think of anyone right now. Like my wife said, Kim didn't go out a lot and when she did it was always with her friends. I just don't understand why she didn't tell us. We could have dealt with it together. It wouldn't have been the ideal situation but we would have dealt with it."

"I can understand that. When I get any new information I will let you know."

Rebecca and Lisa came back with a small book. It was black with gold lettering and a small ribbon marking the last page written. Rebecca lovingly ran her fingers over the velvety cover as if her touch would bring to life the author of it's many pages. Reluctantly she handed the book to Lieutenant Darby.

"Can I have it back when you are done with it? I don't know that I can ever bring myself to read it but I would like to keep it."

"I promise I will get it back to you as soon as possible. Is there anything else I can do for you right now? I am available any time you need me for questions. We will solve this. It might take a little while but we are all going to do what we can to get you some answers for Kim's sake."

"Thank you for coming out here today. Do you know when they will release Kim to us? It would mean a lot just to be able to say goodbye to her." Rebecca's voice broke and Jim quickly took her in his arms his own eyes filling with tears.

Mike swallowed a lump before answering, "I can get that information from the coroner's office when I get back to the office. I will call you as soon as I know."

He went to the door while the Chaplain gave some encouraging words to the Short's. As soon as he was back in his car, he let out a shaky breath. He wondered how much more this couple would have to suffer before this case was over. If it were up to him, Kim would get her justice and her parents would get some peace.

....

The police were about to get a strange visit and some unexpected aid that would divide the departments opinions.

Chapter 5

March 15th, 2007

Diary,
Today for the first time in my life, I lied to my parents. I didn't realize how hard it would be to look my mom in the eye and tell her I was going to the library. I'm just not ready to tell them about Sean yet. It's still too new and to be honest, I'm not sure how Dad would take it. They still think of me as a little girl and I'm not little anymore.

Sean met me at the river. We walked along the beach just talking. When he holds my hand I feel like I'm floating, my feet never touch the ground. Sean is the first guy who hasn't asked me to have sex the first time we go out. I've told him my dreams and he understands why I want to wait. But, ooh it is so hard to say no to those beautiful eyes.

. . . .

April 30th, 2007

Diary,

What have I done? I'm still shaking inside. Sean and I made love for the first time. It was exciting, yet scary, sweet, yet emotional. He was very gentle with me (as if he would be anything else). It was a little different than I thought it would be. Everyone told me it would hurt but it wasn't that bad. It was a little uncomfortable at first but I got used to it pretty quick.

I know I am in love. I've asked Sean to come and meet Mom and Dad. He's a little shy, though. I think he's afraid of Dad and what he'd do if he found out what we've done. I've told him not to worry, that they'll love him just as much as me but he doesn't believe me. I'll ask him again tomorrow.

. . . .

July 29th, 2007

Diary,

My life is over. Sean is gone, told me not to call him again, he doesn't want to see me anymore. How could he? I feel so used. Like a tissue you wipe your nose on and then toss away. But he's not just tossing me away. Now he's throwing away his child.

I should be about 3 months by now. I've waited this long to make sure I truly am pregnant. I went to the Health Department this morning. It was strange to watch the lines turn blue on the stick. To think, right now I have a baby growing inside me. What will it be, a boy or a girl? What will it look like? How in the world am I going to tell Mom and Dad?

I haven't said anything to anyone yet except Sean. As soon as I found out I called him. I thought he would be surprised but I never thought he would say the things he did. He said he didn't want a kid and he didn't want to see me anymore. He told me he wasn't even sure it was his. As if it could be anyone else's.

Sean is the only boy I have ever been with and the only one I have ever loved.

The lady at the Health Department said that if I wanted an abortion that it wasn't too late. I told her no way. I know it isn't what I had planned but I can't help but think of how funny it will be to have a baby of my own. There is no way I could kill an innocent baby. And I really don't want to give it up either. I just don't know.

Right now I can't think straight. I don't know what to do or who to turn to. I wish Kelly were here. I miss her. Oh, God, what have I done? What have I done?

....

Mike Darby sat for a moment longer looking at the small book before closing it softly. The first rule of homicide investigations is don't let it get personal. But right now, he felt about as up close and personal as you could get. Reading the innermost thoughts of that young girl brought home the reality that someone had taken not only her chances at life but also snuffed out the life of an innocent baby who never had a chance. Mike wanted to find that person really badly. He also wanted to talk to Sean. If that boy was as cold hearted as to use Kim the way it appeared he had, he just might be cold enough to be a killer. Mike was going to find out.

Cooper was sitting outside the door of the interrogation rooms when Mike came up.

"Have the boys said any more than they did yesterday?"

Cooper smiled, "Nope. Neither one wanted to carry on a conversation and after me putting on all my charms too. Seems a night away from mommy has 'em forgetting how to talk."

Mike looked in the small window of Interrogation Room 2 to judge by body language which boy he wanted to talk to first. After seeing Sean laid back in his chair with his eyes closed, Mike decided he'd start with him.

As the door opened, Sean jerked upright in his chair mentally preparing for what would come next. He hadn't slept much the night before, thoughts and visions of a beautiful girl with blood all over her keeping him up. He had gotten to talk to Bobby for a little bit, though. Bobby said he hadn't told them anything different than Sean had. So the police had lied to him then. He'd remember that next time.

Mike sat down across the table from Sean trying to get some sense of who this boy was. It wasn't long before Sean was getting fidgety from the scrutiny.

"Why don't you start asking me again if I did it instead of just staring at me? I mean, I know I'm still wearing the same thing as yesterday when you saw me so it's not my outfit you're looking at."

Mike took a deep breath. "How'd you sleep?"

"Like a log. Any other questions?"

"Sean, you can drop the attitude, it won't get you any points. If we're going to get to the bottom of this, we've got to be straight up with each other."

"So telling me my best friend lied about me and said I killed that girl is being straight up? I didn't think so. Nothing I say is going to matter anyway. Ya'll have us pegged for this so you can do whatever you want to make it look like we did. I'm just waiting for my parents to come and get me."

"Sean, do you know how many times we got a confession from a person who we know had committed the crime, all by saying their buddy gave them up? That's just good police work. Let's talk about the girl again. Are you sure you've never met her before?"

"I told you no. I've never met her."

"If I showed you her picture again, do you think you might remember?"

"No. Believe me, I remember exactly what she looks like. I spent all last night seeing her face. It's not something I'll likely forget. But that don't change the fact that I don't know her."

"So if I tell you we've got some evidence that she was dating a boy named Sean, what would you say?"

"I'd say check out another Sean because it wasn't me."

"And if I told you that we have DNA evidence that says this Sean had sex with her, what would you say then?"

"I'd say bring it because this Sean didn't know her, date her, or have sex with her. But like I said, ya'll can make the evidence say whatever you want and there ain't a thing I can do about it."

"We can't change DNA evidence, we only match it. And if it comes back to you, there won't be anything you can do about it. A judge and jury will take one look at it and put you in jail for the rest of your life. I don't know, though, we do have the death penalty in Arkansas so you may have that to look forward to."

"It won't happen. I didn't do it."

"ok You just sit tight. I'm going next door to talk to your friend and see if last night might have jogged his memory."

Mike got up and shut the door with a click. Sean sat there looking at the door wondering if the evil forces conspiring against him were laughing right now at the chaos he was in. He sure as hell wasn't laughing.

....

A few doors down, Olen was sorting through the autopsy report sent over by the coroner. Olen never did understand why they had to put so much medical jargon in these reports. It just meant you had to explain it all to a jury anyway. The report did say that the coroner obtained a DNA sample from the fetus. That would help pin point the father. Who knew how long it would take to get the results, though. The State Crime Lab in Little Rock was usually backed up for months on DNA. Of course, the DNA just gave a profile. You had to have a suspect to match it with. Olen wondered if they already had their match sitting in interrogation.

He was interrupted in his thoughts by a knock on the door. Marsha, the secretary, stuck her head in the door.

"Sir, you have a visitor. She says she has some information on the murder."

"Send her in. Round up Mike if you can find him and send him in."

"Sure thing."

A lady stepped into his office looking very uncomfortable. Olen was stunned at his first sight of her. She was petite, about 5'1" on tip toe, with skin the color of caramel oozing from a Snickers Bar. Her jet black hair was braided with wisps of curls coming loose around her ears. Her brown, doe eyes looking at him made goose bumps on Olen's skin, giving the impression that she was peering into his deepest soul. But what shocked Olen the most was the silvery scar running from one side of her throat to the other. He had the feeling that this lady shouldn't be here talking to him, she should be a ghost.

Her voice startled him from his contemplations making him blush like a teenage boy caught looking at a Playboy magazine.

"You are the chief? The one who is finding this girl's killer?"

Olen stood abruptly. "Yes ma'am. I am Olen Brown, Chief Deputy." Olen put out his hand. The ghostly sensation traveled up his arm as she took his hand. Yet her touch was warm, putting to rest his fears of dealing with a spirit.

"I am Evangeline. I was expecting someone else. You do not look like the man in my vision."

Olen didn't know what to say to this so he just stared at the woman in front of him.

"I have information for you. I have seen this death. This young girl, she is waiting to cross over. Her soul is not at peace. You must find the man who lives in white but underneath is dressed all in black."

"Ms. Evangeline, are you saying you saw this girl being murdered? You saw who did this?"

"I have seen it in my dream. I have not seen his face. He keeps it concealed from me."

Another knock came at the door. Mike made his way into the office glancing first at Olen and then at the lady still standing in front of his desk.

"You wanted to see me, sir?"

Olen introduced Mike to Evangeline and watched his face as he took her hand. Olen was pleased to note that Mike, too, was affected by this woman.

"Ms. Evangeline says she knows something about our murder case. Can you tell me exactly what you saw and when?"

"I must first tell you, I do not usually tell people of my visions. I have learned in life, people are very wary of the unknown. They cannot see beyond what they can hold in their hands, touch it, smell it, taste it. My mother was Creole. She taught me that there are some things in life that cannot be explained but must be felt in your very soul. Many times I have had these visions and they have always been true. Sometimes they are not so easy to understand and may take many months before I can realize what they mean.

This vision came to me last night. I could see a young girl with a piece of paper in her hand, trees all around her. I could hear the sound of water but it was not a soothing sound. It was a frightful sound as if the water was going to overtake her. She was unafraid yet I sensed a sadness in her. She repeatedly wrote the same words on the paper until there was no more room. Then I saw the sun grow dark and a man coming behind her. On one side of the man, he wore white, coming up to her with his hands outstretched. As she turned to him still unafraid, his clothes dropped from him and then there was blackness enveloping both of them. All I could see clearly were his hands and the paper. The man held two things in his hands, one I could not see. The girl seemed confused until she saw the knife in his hands. She tried to pull free of the blackness but the knife plunged down. The paper fell to the ground and my vision lifted. Later, I was able to see a man, not the man with the blackness, picking up the girl and lifting her to freedom. She was at peace in his arms. This is the man I was seeking today."

Olen and Mike sat stunned. Neither seemed able to come up with a reply until Evangeline spoke again.

"You must find the man with the double soul. He is a wolf walking among the sheep. No one sees him for his true self."

"Forgive me for not understanding everything you saw. You could not see his face?" Olen asked.

"No. I saw only his hands and clothing."

"You said you saw her writing. What were the words she was writing?"

"She only wrote two words again and again, 'Forgive Me'."

Suddenly the door opened and Malone stepped into the crowded room. Unaware of the drama around him, Malone spoke to Olen. "I've searched all the area around the crime scene and I can't find a knife anywhere. Unless you want to call out divers, I don't see how we're going to find it."

A sharp indrawn breath came from Evangeline. Her eyes were solidly fixed on Malone as he spoke.

"You! You are the one. You will release her. I have seen it."

Malone looked at her as if she was the bearded lady in the circus.

"What are you talking about? I ain't holding anybody, how am I suppose to release 'em?"

"I'll explain it all later. Malone, this is Evangeline. She is here trying to help us with this case."

Malone didn't look like he thought she would be much help. He let out something close to a snort and looked back at the Chief. Evangeline was having trouble looking away from Malone. Her intense stare soon got to him and he started trying to ease himself behind Mike. Mike seemed to find this hilarious and tried hard not to start laughing at the giant of a man shrinking from a woman who didn't even reach his elbow.

Evangeline took Olen's hand and placed a small paper in his palm. She turned to leave and spoke softly once more.

"You must find the paper. If you find it, you will find the evil. The knife has been washed clean. It will do you little good. Find the paper."

She left slowly from the room, seeming to take the warmth from it as she went. All those in the room felt a sense of loss unlike anything they had known before. The only sign of her visit was the slip of paper with an address on it that she had left in the hands of the Chief.

Chapter 6

Y ou can't tell me you believe all that hokey she was spewing. It's all a bunch of voodoo mumbo jumbo if you ask me."

"Come on Malone, you know you're just afraid she's going to end up putting a spell on you. Looks to me like she already has." Mike smiled again at the vision of Malone being scared of a little slip of a Creole girl.

"She just gives me the shivers is all." Malone still couldn't shake the memory of Evangeline's eyes staring at him. Women didn't have much place in Malone's life and he preferred it that way. All they did was start trouble whenever they were around.

Olen broke in, "I think we should go back over what she said. Whether or not we believe in her visions, she did know a few things about the scene. Unless we think she may have been involved, which I seriously doubt, we have to believe she got the information some how. Maybe she is protecting someone."

Olen still couldn't make up his mind about her. He looked again at the address on his desk. Had Evangeline given them the address to the killer, which was a little too much to hope for, or was this her address? At the time, he hadn't even thought about asking her for her address and phone number so they could get back in touch with her.

First things first.

"Malone, drive out to this address and see what you can find out. If it is Evangeline's at least we'll know where to contact her."

Malone looked uneasy. "Chief, if you don't mind, I'd prefer Mike to check it out. I, uh, had something else I needed to go do."

Mike couldn't control the laughter. Malone shot him a look that should have had Mike shaking in his boots. It didn't. Mike knew Malone too well. Down deep, Malone was like a pit bull with half a set of dentures, all bark and no bite.

Olen sighed, wondering what he'd done to deserve such a headache.

"I need Mike here to talk to the boys and their parents. I'm going to see Judge Marshall about a search warrant for both homes. You're the only one I have that I trust. Plus, Evangeline seemed to think you were going to solve this somehow. See if you can get her to remember anything else from her "dream" that we can make sense of."

Malone grumbled something about women and trouble before snatching the address from the desk. The door rattled on it's hinges as Malone left, the two men smiling as they thought about being a fly on the wall during that interview.

Olen looked at Mike and asked,

"What do you think, Mike, all kidding aside? Do you think she really has something here?"

"I don't know. I've never really thought of psychics being anything more than fortune tellers, using their crystal ball to tell young girls about meeting their dream man. She seemed sincere and she did have some interesting facts about the scene. She may have seen or heard on the news some of it, but we haven't told anyone except the family how Kim died. Evangeline did mention the knife."

"Yeah, I caught that, too. I can't really see her as our killer. It could be a ploy to lead us off track, if she knows who did it. What do you think about her personally? That scar is interesting. I've never seen anyone with a cut like that who wasn't in the morgue."

"It might be a good idea to see what we can find on her. I agree, she didn't get that scar without some kind of record of it. I'll go look her up in the state files. I'd better check the national registry too. She did say she's Creole. Chances are she spent some time in Louisiana."

"Yeah, dig up anything you can. Have you talked to the two boys again?"

"Just Sean. Oh, I totally forgot, with our visitor and all, I've read Kim's diary. It has some information we can use. She was seeing a boy named Sean, who also happens to be the father of her child. He dumped her when he found out about the baby. I think it is too much of a coincidence that one of our suspects just happens to have the same name."

"Is he admitting to knowing her?"

"No. He still says he's never seen her before. He's angry and defensive so I can't get him to talk to me much. I was just on my way to talk to Bobby when Marsha came to get me."

"Okay. Go talk to him then see what you can find on Evangeline. I'll be back as soon as I talk to Judge Marshall."

....

Bobby was tired. Tired of sitting, tired of worrying, tired of everything. He just wanted this to be over, like a bad dream he could wake up from. He wondered when his mom was coming to get him and how his little sister was doing.

The door opened and Bobby looked up to see a detective come in. At least it wasn't the guy who had come to get them. He was as irritating as a mosquito.

Mike sat down across from Bobby, putting a cup of water down in front of him. Bobby took the cup, absently wiping the drops from the rim.

"Hi, Bobby. I'm Lieutenant Mike Darby. Are you okay? Do you need anything"

"No, I'm fine, thanks."

"Do you mind if I ask you some more questions about the girl?"

"I don't know what else I can tell you about her. I didn't know her."

"Well, we have some more information that came out last night. It seems she was dating a boy named Sean. Don't you think that's kind of coincidental, her dating a boy named Sean and us finding a boy named Sean at the scene of her murder?"

"It wasn't Sean Fisher. Sean doesn't have a girlfriend right now. He was seeing Kathy Shaw but they broke up about a month ago."

"Do you think he could have been seeing this girl on the side without telling you?"

Bobby laughed, a soft laugh. "No sir. We don't blow our noses without telling each other. Sean and I have been friends forever. If he was dating someone, I knew about it before she did."

"Okay. Let's go back over the scene again. What was the first thing you saw when you walked into the clearing?"

"I saw the girl. She was laying there kind of on her side, kind of face down, with blood all around her. I wasn't even thinking when I bent down to touch her. I just wanted to see if she was ok Sean reached down and grabbed my hand and said 'Don't'. His face was already turning white. See, Sean doesn't like blood at all. It makes him sick. He wouldn't say anything to you about it, though. He thinks it makes him weak or something."

"Did you notice anything else around her, maybe a piece of paper, a pen or pencil?"

Bobby wrinkled his brow, trying to remember back to the ground around Kim. "No, I don't remember seeing anything. I really didn't have much time to see anything before all those girls came in and started screaming."

Mike continued writing in his notebook before asking,

"When you and Sean were going in, did you notice any areas that had already been walked on, you know, with brush broken or tramped down?"

"I didn't really think about it I guess. But it did seem pretty easy going. I think that is why we were so quiet getting in, everything was already pushed out of the way."

"Do you remember hearing anything unusual, maybe footsteps or twigs breaking?"

"Not that I remember. It was quiet, I don't even remember birds chirping or anything." He paused before asking, "She hadn't been dead long, had she? She was still warm when I touched her."

"No. She hadn't." Mike didn't want to say how long because he still wasn't sure if he was getting the full story or not. He was beginning to think, though, that these boys, at least this one, was being truthful. Which made him wonder where they went from here?

"So, whoever did this was out there, with us? He could have been watching us the whole time." Bobby gave a little shudder at the thought of how close they had been to dying. What if whoever killed the girl had decided to get rid of them, too? He didn't want to think about it. They had been so stupid. For a simple prank, this could have cost them more than they were already paying. It's funny how quick you can grow up. Bobby was thinking about his Mom and little sister. They depend on him to be the man of the house and now he wasn't even there for them. He had let them down. He promised himself, if he got out of this, he wouldn't ever let them down again.

"Bobby, this girl, she wasn't just some girl, she was somebody's daughter. She had a future ahead of her, a life to live. Someone took that from her. I need to know who that someone is. Kim deserves that much. Her parents deserve that much."

"Sir, I swear to you, if I knew who did it, I would tell you. We didn't do it. No matter what you may think of us, we would never do this. Sean likes to act tough sometimes but he's just as scared as I am. I just want to go home, to take care of my family."

Mike saw and heard the sincerity in his voice and for the first time believed without a doubt, this boy was telling the truth. Years of police work had taught him to read people. This kid wasn't involved with this murder. He was one of those caught in the wrong place at the wrong time.

Mike stood up gathering his papers.

"ok I'll see about bringing your mother in as soon as I can. If you need anything, knock on this door and Cooper will get it for you."

Bobby doubted that Cooper would even answer him much less get him anything he needed. What he needed most, Cooper couldn't give him anyway. Peace of mind was something you had to give yourself.

....

Judge Marshall signed the search warrants for the residents of both Sean Fisher and Bobby Timmons, giving the police full rights to search every nook and cranny of the homes. If there was any evidence to be found, the police would find it. Since they were looking for anything that could link these boys to Kim, just about everything was included in the search warrant. Unless it was bigger than an elephant, it was admissible to search.

Olen next set up a bail hearing for that afternoon for both boys. He didn't know what he wanted from that. Both boys seemed to have stable homes so he wasn't really afraid of either skipping town before a trial. With this crime being so sensational in the news, neither Sean nor Bobby would make a step without someone reporting on it. Olen didn't like sensations any more than the Sheriff did but sometimes they could be an asset to the police.

As he walked back to his car, Olen wondered how Malone was making out with Evangeline. He hoped Malone was being civil.

....

Malone was sitting in his truck staring at the address on the paper. He looked up again at the numbers on the house in front of him. Sighing, he knew he couldn't put it off any longer. Hell, she was probably in there right now "seeing" him with her damn vision. Crazy woman.

He stepped out, took a deep breath and walked up the steps to the door. He had taken the time to take stock of his surroundings. The house sat back from the road with a wooden fence surrounding the tree lined walkway. Flowers and all sorts of greenery were abundant in a stone garden beside the house.

The house itself was a small, rustic cabin with a wrap around porch. A wooden swing overlooked the garden area leaving one to feel at peace here. He could see where a woman such as Evangeline would make a home here. It was evident she had been abused in some way in the past, so this was probably her sanctuary.

Malone's knock was answered by Evangeline along with a small shepherd with icy blue eyes. Malone stared at the dog waiting for the inevitable barking that usually accompanied such animals. None came. Evangeline stood waiting, Malone knew she was waiting but for the life of him he didn't know what for.

Malone cleared his throat, "Uh, hello Ms. The Chief wanted me to come talk to you again. We weren't real sure if this was your address or not."

"Did you think I had done your work for you and given you the address of your killer?" Evangeline smiled. "Come in, then, I know you will want some answers to your many questions. I will see if I can answer them."

She stepped back and led Malone to a small living room. The room was nothing as Malone would have imagined. He had envisioned incense burning and shrunken heads or something. Instead, the furniture was soft colors, blues with yellow flower designs on the sofa and chair. A rocking chair sat in one corner with a wicker basket on the floor beside it. The pictures on the wall were of children. One in particular caught Malone's eye. It was of a small boy and girl playing around a sand box. There was a woman sitting near the children on a swing, her laughing face caught in the sunlight. It was Evangeline. But who were the children?

"Did you want to ask me questions?"

Evangeline's voice brought Malone back to the present time. He didn't have time to be delving into the past of this woman. He was trying to solve a murder. Yet, one question he couldn't stop himself from asking.

"Where is the T.V.?"

His question must have confused her. She wasn't expecting him to notice her possessions. Good, he thought. Let her be just as shaken up as he was.

"I do not have a television. I prefer to hear the sound of silence to the sound of man's inhumanity to other men. I live a simple life, Detective. I do not need much to sustain me."

"Then you ain't like any woman I've every met before. They could have a house full of stuff and still want more. Do you live here alone?"

"I have Paix." She pointed to the dog laying beside her feet. Paix looked up to her as if to ask why she called his name. She smiled and softly rubbed the dog's head, the love obvious in her attention.

Malone grunted before bringing things back to the reason he was there. "About the knife, I know I said something about it when I came in back at the office but do you know something else about it?"

"I have told you, I saw it in my vision. It was black handled, not with smooth edges but with ridges. The kind hunters use. The man in black took it with him. He stopped by the water to wash it before wrapping it in his clothing. I do not know where it is now. He also has the paper. He looks at it several times. He is keeping it but I do not know why. It is as if he wants it to remind him of why he killed her. I do not always understand all of my visions. Some have to come to me many times before they become clear."

"Have you had this 'vision' many times?"

"No. Just once. It was very descriptive, though, not fuzzy as some of my visions are. Some begin hazy and then become more clear as time goes on. That is why I came to your Chief. I believe my vision was true. I want this girl's spirit to be free."

"Yeah, you said something about that earlier. What makes you think that it's me that will solve this? I mean, we have lots of officers working on this case, it's not just me."

"I saw you in my vision. You were lifting her up and she felt safe in your arms. Do you not think yourself capable of this?"

Malone shifted a little of his weight from his left leg to his right. His thigh was bothering him from standing so much but he didn't want to sit down. If he sat, she might think he was comfortable here.

"Ma'am, I've solved a lot of cases over the last thirty years, so I figure I can solve this one. I just don't like the idea of you thinking I'm some kind of hero or something."

She looked up at Malone wondering why this man tried so hard to hide his abilities. Evangeline had learned a long time ago how to judge people from the signals they put off. This man liked to believe himself tough, unfeeling, detached. Yet she could sense in him a part that wanted to be needed.

"Sergeant, would you like to sit down? Your leg will feel better if you rest it."

Malone's eyes shot to hers. How in the world did she know about his leg?

"It doesn't take a psychic to notice how you winced when you shifted your weight. I am good at watching people, I have had to be. Please, sit down."

Damn it, now she was reading his mind. He had to get out of here fast, but he still needed to ask her some more questions.

He glanced at his choices of seats and chose the soft chair. He tried to tell himself it wasn't because it was the farthest one away from her but he knew he'd be lying.

"Have you remembered anything else about this man that might help us? How tall he was, how much he weighed, was he a black man or a white man?"

"I did not see his face or body. All I could see clearly were his hands. They are those of a white man. They are smooth, he does not work with his hands. I cannot say how big he was. I am sorry I can not help you more. I am certain that the paper is important. That is what stood out to me."

Malone was quiet for a moment, considering what she had told him. He wanted to ask a few questions about Evangeline's background but didn't know how to go about it. This was a first for him, not being able to interview someone. Instead, he asked something else that was puzzling him.

"Are you sure there was only one man, that it wasn't maybe two men or maybe young boys since his hands weren't rough?"

"I only saw one. It could be that my vision wanted me to focus on the one but it is unlikely. As far as if he was young or old, I couldn't say for sure. The hands were not that of an elderly person but I could not be sure of his age."

"For that matter, how do you know it is a man and not a woman?"

"No, it was not a woman. The feelings I received from the killer were those of a man. I do not know how to explain how I can tell, I just can."

"ok If you think of anything else will you call and let us know?"

"Yes. If I have another vision, I will tell you. I do not have a telephone but I will come to you."

"You don't have a phone either? What if something happens and you need the police or an ambulance? How are you going to get help?"

"If it is God's will that something happens to me, a telephone would not save me."

"What kind of fool thing is that to say? You live out here in the back of nowhere without a phone or a T.V. and nobody but a dog for company! You've got to have some way to communicate with the rest of the world."

A look of sadness and maybe a little fear crossed her face before she could mask it from Malone. Damn, he hadn't meant to be so abrupt with her or to scare her but he guessed he had.

"Sergeant, I have lived among everyone else and shared that world. I believe having no one is better than having the wrong one."

She stood up and led him to the door. Malone realized he had crossed the line between an interview and a personal attack but he wasn't sure how to apologize. For some reason, he didn't want to leave with her upset with him. That shook him more than her visions or her ability to read him like a book.

He walked to the door but as he was stepping out onto the porch he turned.

"Ma'am, I'm sorry for what I said. It's none of my business how you live your life. I shouldn't have gotten so loud. It's just that-"

"It is alright. I realize I must seem strange to you but I cannot change who I am. Maybe someday you will understand."

She shut the door before Malone could reply. He stood for a moment looking at the door. He knew she wasn't coming back to open it again but still he waited. For the first time in his life, Malone felt alone. He turned away from her door feeling like what he needed most was right behind him.

Chapter 7

Judge Marshall set bail at $100,000 each for Sean Fisher and Bobby Timmons. Linda Timmons found a bail bondsman who put up the bail for Bobby. Richard and Candy Fisher cashed out a savings account set aside for Sean's college fund. Both boys were on their way home.

At another home in Malvern, Kimberly Short's parents were setting up funeral arrangements for their daughter. The coroner had released her body for burial. Everything that could be learned from DNA and the body itself was preserved in evidence, the rest was up to the police to determine.

The media had finally given up getting anything new on the case and had set off for a new breaking story on a government scandal in North Little Rock. The 5 o'clock news would carry only a brief summary of the case for it's viewers. Some were moving on. Life in the small town should have been returning to some sense of normalcy. Yet how could anything ever return to the way it should be?

The police department itself was seeing a change. The detectives had hit a dead end. They had lots of tips that turned out to be a wild goose chase. They also had the usual batch of helpful citizens who called in to say they saw the boys kill Kim. The problem was the eyewitnesses swore the boys raped her and beat her as she lay screaming on the ground.

Mike Darby and Doug Shankles were in full agreement that the killer was still out there laughing at them. Cooper really didn't care one way or the other who killed her. He just wanted someone to interrogate. Chief Brown knew he was going to have to do something soon about Cooper but what to do was the question. Olen had only put up with him this long because Cooper was the Sheriff's nephew. He was a lawsuit waiting to happen. Olen didn't need that in his department.

Then there was Malone. No one knew what had happened that afternoon at Evangeline's, Malone wouldn't talk about it. He wasn't talking much at all. All they could get from him was that she didn't know anything more than what she had already told them. Olen and Mike were both worried about Malone but they respected his space and his privacy. They could only stand back and hope that once this case was solved, their old Malone would return to them.

....

On Monday, August 13th, Kimberly Short was laid to rest at Pine View Cemetery. One hundred and seventy five people crowded into the church where Kim had been baptized to pay their respect and say goodbye. Students and teachers from Malvern High school huddled together, mourning the loss of one of their own. Mothers hugged their daughters close, tears flowing freely.

Jim and Rebecca Short sat holding each other as they listened to Reverend Peterson talk about Kim's life. He told of a smiling child who had always made the church a little brighter. Her innocence had truly made her a child of God. The Reverend concluded by quoting Romans 6:23-"For the wages of sin is death; but the gift of God is eternal life through Jesus Christ our Lord," before asking everyone to join him in a silent prayer to send Kim's spirit home.

As the church emptied, the Shorts realized that even among the crowd, they were alone. Both had pictured growing old together with grandchildren to keep them company. Now all their hopes lay in a mahogany casket deep below the ground.

Bobby Timmons mourned the death of Kim in his own way. Gone was the young prankster who's only care was if his little sister got into his stuff without asking. Bobby's responsibilities to his family pushed him to get a summer job at the local animal shelter. Taking care of the animals enabled him to escape the prying eyes and behind-the-hand whispers he got every time he went to the grocery store. He couldn't help but wish all this was over so he could prove to everyone he wasn't a killer.

Sean had turned into an angry, cynical young man. Lashing out at anyone and everyone, his parents were at a loss as to what to do. Since Bobby had gotten a job, Sean didn't have anyone to talk to so his pent up emotions had no where to go. Candy watched her son with a breaking heart wishing she could kiss away his hurt as she had his skinned knees as a child. Richard watched them both waste away with worry and thought of how he would love to get his hands on whoever had killed that girl. In his eyes, the killer had destroyed more than one life that day.

....

He was washing the knife in the cool water close to the bank. The cleansing strokes he made only helped him justify the kill. No one else would understand, he knew, but he was calm. His steps were unhurried as he walked toward the road where his car was waiting. He couldn't go back the way he had come in because he had heard the screams and knew she had been found.

Tucking the small piece of paper into the pocket of his shirt, he thought of how easy it had been. When Kim had told him about the baby, a surprising anger had set in. Why had she spoiled everything by letting herself get into that mess? He couldn't let anyone find out.

The hardest part had been when she looked up at him. She had smiled at first, trusting him, until she saw the knife. That confused her. The first thrust he had hesitated on before he willed himself to finish it. Now it was done and she wouldn't let him down again.

. . . .

Evangeline woke with a start, a scream catching in her throat. Her hands were cold yet sweat beaded on her forehead, clinging her hair to her face. She always hated this part. Waking from a vision was like coming out of amnesia. She took a minute to familiarize herself with her surroundings before her heartbeat returned to normal.

Rising from her bed, she went into the kitchen for a glass of ice water. Her throat was dry and she still trembled as she took a drink. With the vision still fresh on her mind, she tried to sort out what she'd seen. The killer had been clearer this time although he still hadn't shown his face. Sighing she realized she would have to go into town and face Sergeant Malone again and the demons he had brought to the surface on his last visit.

. . . .

When Mike Darby saw Evangeline walk into the police department, his first thought was, thank God. The search of the boy's homes had turned up nothing. That hadn't surprised him. What did was how quickly this case had hit a dead end. No one had come forward with any tips. Usually in a murder investigation, they would have several people willing to snitch on their buddy if they thought there would be a reward. No one in the town seemed to have any real information. Except for the mystical lady who had just walked through the door.

His next thought was, where is Malone. He wanted to see how the two reacted to each other. For the life of him he couldn't figure out what had went wrong. He had done everything he could to goad Malone into one his famous tempers but Malone refused to be baited. Mike missed that.

Evangeline too seemed to be looking for him. When she didn't see him in the room, she seemed to lose some of her tension. She hadn't realized how tightly she was grabbing her purse until her fingers started tingling. Relaxing, she saw Mike and headed in his direction. Maybe Malone wouldn't be here and she could leave without a confrontation.

Mike smiled to her as she walked up. He had been unable to find any information on her in the computers. Of course it would be helpful if he had her last name. It would seem that Evangeline was a popular name in Louisiana. He promised himself to get her full name before she left.

"Ms. Evangeline, it's nice to see you again. Would you like to sit down?"

"Thank you. I have some more information for you. Another vision came to me last night. It started the same as the first but became more clear. I could see things from the eyes of the man who killed the girl."

"Tell me what you saw. Wait. Do you mind if I round up the Chief and the other deputies? Then we can all hear it first hand."

Evangeline looked uncertain but finally said, "That is fine. I will wait."

Mike went to find Olen first. He found him talking to the Sheriff.

"Chief, I think you need to come down here. Evangeline is back and has some more info for us. Do you know where Malone and Doug are?"

"Doug is over at the prosecutors office again. I'm not sure about Malone. Last time I saw him he was sorting through records. I'll try to find him. You get back to her before she gets cold feet and makes a run for it."

"ok Don't let him weasel out of this. We need to find out what happened between those two."

"I know. Malone needs to face up to whatever is bugging him."

Mike went back to his office to find Evangeline looking at the pictures on his desk.

"That's my pride and joy. She's three now but thinks she's thirty. Of course Daddy might play a part in that. She has me wrapped so far around her finger, I'll never get loose."

"She is beautiful. What is her name?"

"Amanda. She looks just like her mother."

"I can see why you would be proud. Cherish her while you can."

Mike saw a look of sadness cross her eyes before she sat back down. He really didn't know what to say so he started getting his notebook out. With relief, Olen and Malone came in to break the silence. Malone didn't look at Evangeline at first. She couldn't take her eyes off him. Olen took her hand and told her how nice it was to see her again. Malone finally looked at her. Both Olen and Mike could feel without a doubt the connection bouncing between the two.

Olen cleared his throat.

"Mike tells me you have some more information for us."

Evangeline broke the eye contact with Malone.

"Yes. Another vision came to me last night. It was much like the first only this time I could see from the killer's eyes. He was washing the knife in the water and thinking of her. He was relieved he had killed her. He believes he is justified because of her pregnancy. He sees it as some sort of betrayal. He has anger towards her at first but then feels happy it is over. He puts the paper in his pocket. His car is waiting on a road not far from the body. He is still nearby when the others find her. He hears screams. The car is red, a small car that looks like a Toyota."

"Could you see a license plate on the car? Maybe even a few letters or numbers?", Mike asked.

"No. All I could see was the color and size. I am sorry I cannot tell you more."

"That's ok You have told us a lot that will help us. Could you see her in your vision? What she was doing or saying?" Mike was writing as he asked.

"I could see her. She was writing on the paper when he came up. She was concentrating on the paper and did not hear his footsteps. When she saw him, she seemed a little surprised yet unconcerned. The knife confused her until he raised it. He covers her mouth and turns her to where she has her back up against his chest. He hesitates for a moment before raising the knife again and again."

"How many times did he stab her?"

"Seven times the knife comes down. She tried to fight but he is too strong for her."

Malone is the first to notice the tears falling from Evangeline's eyes. He moves over to her and hands her a tissue. She glances up to see the apology in his face. With an unspoken word, she forgives him. Malone sits back down to stare at his hands.

Olen asks her, "Can you give us any idea as to who this man is?"

"No. Only that he is disappointed in her for something. Emotions are not always clear in my visions but his are very strong. I do not think this man is capable of controlling his emotions. I fear if he feels this way again, he would kill again. His mind is so unstable."

"We need to find him soon. Mike, are we for certain that one of these boys didn't do this and the other is covering for him?"

"Chief, I would bet my best fishing pole that neither one of those boys are our killer."

"Well, then, we've got some work to do. If Ms. Evangeline says he will kill again, then we need to get him off the streets. We really do appreciate all your help. I'm afraid this case hasn't been leading anywhere as of yet. Do you think you will have more visions like this one?"

"I do not know. Sometimes I have the same vision over and over yet other times I only have it once. I will let you know if I see anything else."

She got up and moved toward the entrance. Mike realized he still hadn't got Evangeline's last name. He stood up and walked beside her. "Ms. Evangeline, can you tell me your full name, in case I need to get back in touch with you?"

She hesitated before answering, "It is insignificant. If you need anything, you have my address. I need to be going now. I do hope you catch this man. Good day."

Malone moved quickly to intercept her. He placed his hand on her arm which startled her. He jerked it away so as not to frighten her any more than he already had. Sometimes he hated being so big.

"Can I walk you out? I would like to talk to you."

"Yes, I would like your company."

Once outside, Malone slowed his gait so she could easily keep up. He would have to remember how small she was.

"I wanted to tell you how sorry I am about the other day. I was way out of line and I had no right to question how you live. My job has always been to protect people and I'm afraid I let it lead me to butt into things that don't concern me."

"I have forgiven you, Sergeant. Life is too short to stay angry. Life should be enjoyed every day if for no other reason than it could be our last day in this world."

"Ben. My name is Ben. I would like it if you would call me by it."

"Thank you, Ben. I would like it too."

Evangeline unlocked her car door and slid into the seat. She knew she should be on her way, yet, she lingered for a moment longer. Malone watched her, wondering if she would be coming back. He didn't try to stop her as she closed the door and backed out of the parking lot. It meant a lot to him that she had forgiven him.

Unknown to both of them, two faces were pressed up against a window watching their every move. Mike smiled at the thought of the things he could say when Malone got back in. If his eyes didn't deceive him, Malone just might be goaded into a snarl when he came back in. Mike couldn't wait to try.

Chapter 8

Doug Shankles was riled up. How someone could be so stupid he just couldn't figure out. The Prosecutor sat there behind his desk with a I-don't-care-what-you-think look on his face. Doug wanted to smack it off him.

"I'm trying to tell you, the evidence just won't support a trial of these two boys. The only thing linking them in any way to the murder is them being there when she was found." Doug was trying to be patient.

"That's a whole lot of evidence to my way of thinking. All I have to do is tell the jury how they were leaning over that poor girls bleeding body and they'll hang them."

"While your at it, are you going to tell the jury about the nine teenage girls that were found at the scene, too? Maybe the jury would like to hang them too."

Steve Kooley sat forward in his chair. "I don't appreciate your humor in this situation. This is a serious matter and I am trying to perform my job to the best of my abilities, and that job means protecting the citizens of this town from murderers out to kill our children."

"Save it for the campaign trail, Steve. These boys are not who you are looking for. We are still searching for the person responsible. We have a few leads we are working on." Doug hoped the lie didn't show in his face.

"And I say we already know who did it. The town expects me to charge somebody quickly so they can sleep at night. I'm going to go with what I have. If the police want to help us get a conviction, you need to get me some more evidence, like the murder weapon. I don't care how you get it."

"So, you'd rather fabricate evidence and wrongfully convict two innocent teenagers than wait a little while so we can do our job properly? If I didn't know better I'd say it's an election year. We'll send over any real evidence we get. I personally won't be a part of a mob lynching." Doug stood up to leave.

"You might want to reconsider your attitude, Deputy. Your sheriff is up for re-election too. One little hint of impropriety on the part of his staff and he'll let you go so fast you won't know which way is up."

"I'll take my chances. If you send an innocent boy away, your career won't be smelling like roses either."

Doug left the Prosecutor's office and headed for his car. Sitting in the driver's seat, he tried to think of where he should go first. He didn't think anything he had to say would help the mood at the office right now. He decided to go do a little investigating himself. There had to be someone who knew who Kim was dating. Girls always had friends they told secrets to. Doug wanted to find one.

．．．

Reverend Peterson stopped by to see Jim and Rebecca Short. Both had not been to church since Kim's death. The Reverend was worried. The Short's had always been one of his most loyal parishioners. He had seen a lot of different reactions to death in his years in the church. Some drew closer to God after a loved one died, both as a way to cope and as a way to stay close to the one they lost. Others drifted away, unable to understand why a God of love would take their loved one from them. He hoped that the Shorts were not feeling that way.

Jim answered the door, fatigue apparent in every line of his face. The last thing he wanted right now was to have someone telling him how Kim was in a better place. But he let Reverend Peterson in out of an ingrained sense of hospitality.

"Hello, Reverend. What brings you out this way?"

"I have been worried about you Jim. You and Rebecca haven't been to church and I thought I'd stop by to see if I could help with anything."

"All we need is time, Reverend. We haven't even begun to cope yet."

"Where's Rebecca?"

"She's sleeping. The doctor gave her something to soothe her nerves and help her sleep. She's just exhausted. I guess we both are."

"The church is there to help, Jim. God will never give you anything more than you can bear. Everyone has a cross to carry but God will help you lift it."

"Well, pardon me for saying so Reverend, but God has heaped a pretty heavy cross on us right now. My little girl is gone, my wife cries all the time, refusing to go near Kim's room, and I can't seem to concentrate at work so I end up coming home early every day. I don't think church is at the top of our list right now."

"I'm sorry to hear that. All I've ever wanted to do is help my congregation. Anger at God is not going to help you. Prayer will help you to understand the reasons behind all of God's purposes."

"Are you trying to tell me that there was a purpose to my daughter being killed? Because if you are, I don't think I need your God in my life."

"Jim, I didn't mean it like that. Goodness will come from everything that happens to us in life. Lessons will be learned.

Maybe Kim's death will lead to other girls being protected from such an occurrence."

"Well, I don't see how anything good will come from this and right now I just want to be alone with my wife. If you don't mind, I'd like get some sleep."

Jim opened the door and waited for Reverend Peterson to step through. The Reverend turned once outside to say something more but the door had already closed. Sighing, he thought that not everyone was capable of understanding the glories God could bestow on his people.

....

After five weepy teenage girls, Doug finally found one who could say a complete sentence without using the word "like" and dabbing at her makeup with a tissue. Jessie Stephens was a sophomore at Malvern, a grade above Kim but one of her best friends. Jessie had not been at the river that day, she had been home in bed with bronchitis.

"Did you and Kim hang around the same places?" Doug asked the brown haired girl in front of him.

"Yeah, Kim and I both liked reading so we went to the library a lot. If we weren't there, we were usually hanging out at the river. Kim liked watching the water, she said it made her want to float away."

"Did Kim ever go there with anyone else, a boy maybe?"

Jessie squirmed a little in her chair. She didn't want to snitch on anyone but Kim was dead so she didn't know what it would hurt.

"Yeah, she used to go there with Sean. She didn't tell her parents about him because she said they thought she was too young to date. I don't know when the last time they went there, though. Kim told me they hadn't been able to meet that much lately. Sean had practice on weekends."

"What is Sean's last name? What sport does he play?"

"Branford. He's the quarterback on the football team. He's a real jerk if you ask me but Kim was head over heels in love with him. Most of the girls knew what he was like but no one wanted to tell Kim. She was so naïve, she couldn't tell that he was only after one thing. I think she held him off for a while, though. I tried to talk to her about him a couple of times but she just brushed it off saying he had changed."

"Did she ever tell you they had sex?"

"She kind of hinted at it. I think she wanted to tell me but didn't want me to think bad of her. I could tell something was bothering her that Friday before, well, she died. I asked her what was wrong but she just said 'nothing'. I was coming down with bronchitis or I probably would have pressured her more to talk. I wish I had of."

"It's not your fault. I'm sure she knew you were there for her when she needed you. Do you think this Sean Branford would have hurt her? Had he ever been violent with her in the past?"

"No. Sean was too much of a lover instead of a fighter. He didn't have to use force. He's so cute, girls are falling all over themselves to get to him. He could have just about anyone he wanted. I think that is what appealed to him about Kim. She wasn't drooling all over him. She was kind of like a challenge."

"Was there anyone else do you think, maybe another boy who was jealous of her relationship with Sean?"

"No, Kim only had eyes for Sean. Everyone at school knew it so they didn't bother her."

"ok I appreciate you talking to me. If you think of anything else or hear of anything, call me."

"Sure. I miss Kim. My mom has been watching me like a hawk ever since it happened. I think she is afraid it might happen to me too."

"You can never be too careful, Jessie. Maybe your mom is right to keep you in sight for a while."

"Yeah, none of the girls at school want to go near the river anymore. It used to be the thing to do on the weekend, now, everyone is scared to go out at all."

"Things will get better. We'll find whoever did this. Until then, keep yourself safe."

Doug got up to leave. He looked up to see Jessie's mom leaning on the door, watching them. He smiled at her to let her know he knew what she was feeling. Jessie stayed on the couch, a book laying across her lap.

Doug felt better than he had in a long time. Finally, he felt like they were getting somewhere.

....

Sean Fisher walked into the store with his hands in his pockets. He hated having to go anywhere. People always stared at him, whispering about him as he walked by. Why couldn't they just leave him the hell alone. His mom wanted him to stay at home until all this was settled. He would go stir crazy in that house if he had to stay in it one more day.

He walked over to the cooler to get a Coke. Out of the corner of his eye he saw two kids coming around the end of the aisle. They stopped when they saw him. One was a tall boy with shoulder length blond hair, wearing blue jeans and a t-shirt that had a skull and crossbones on it. The shorter boy was wearing skateboarder shorts and a white shirt with blue stripes. The taller one said something to the other boy before walking up to him.

Sean shut the cooler door and turned to face them.

"Hey, ain't you the one that killed that girl?"

Sean looked from one to the other. He knew he could take the shorter one, he was a pushover. The taller boy though looked a little tougher. With the two of them, he might get a few licks in but he'd probably end up the worse for wear. Oh, what the hell, it would give him something to do.

"I'm talking to you. You deaf or just dumb?"

"Nope. I just don't talk to assholes."

The taller boy stepped forward, Sean didn't back down.

"Hey, you boys! Get out of my store if you're going to start trouble. I don't want any of that in here." The lady at the counter was already reaching for the phone.

Sean looked at both of them and said, "Let's take it outside. I've been itching to have some fun all day.

The three walked out the front door and headed to the back of the parking lot. Sean waited until he thought he could surprise them before spinning around and catching the tall boy on the chin with a right fist. The blow caught the boy off guard and spun him around. The fatter boy came crashing into Sean's stomach, knocking him to the ground. Kicking and hitting his way up, Sean managed to regain his footing. By now the taller boy was back into the fray.

The only sounds were the fists hitting flesh and the grunts when something connected. Sean let all his pent up emotions flow through his hands as he landed blow after blow. Finally, though, his opponents got the upper hand, keeping him pinned down. The taller kid went for Sean's face while his buddy used his feet in Sean's ribs.

With the air knocked out of him, Sean couldn't do much more than lay there and take a beating. Sirens sounded close by, as a police car came barreling through the parking lot. The car screeched to a halt beside the fight. The deputy came running over, yanking hands off Sean's chest.

Sean lay exhausted and bleeding on the ground. But damn, he felt better than he had in weeks.

. . . .

For the second time in less than a month, Richard and Candy Fisher got a call from the Sheriff's office saying they had their son in custody. When the couple walked into the now familiar entrance, Sean was sitting in the hall waiting for them, Cooper sitting across from him. Candy took one look at her son and broke down in tears. Richard really wanted to get a hold of Sean and give him a good thrashing. Maybe if they had given him more of those, they wouldn't be here now.

Sean looked up at his mom and grinned from ear to ear. It might have lifted her spirits if she hadn't also seen the bloody lip, the cuts on his cheeks, and the eye that was already turning black. Sean stood up and hugged Candy.

"Mom, I'm ok, really. I'm sorry you had to come get me again, though."

"Boy, what have you gotten into now?" Richard wasn't going to be swindled by his grin and assurances.

"I got in a fight."

"I can see that. But with who and why?"

Cooper spoke up, "Seems Sean here decided to take on two other boys at one time. He may look rough but you should see the other two."

Richard was surprised at the pride in Cooper's voice. You would have thought it was his son he was talking about.

"Dad, it felt good. I know that sounds dumb but it's true. I just felt all of this anger inside and every time I threw a punch it let some of it go. I didn't even mind taking the hits either. Isn't that weird?"

Richard shook his head but some of his own anger started to leave him, too. Candy was still sniffling into her tissue.

"No, son, that isn't weird." Looking at Cooper he asked, "What do we have to do to take him home?"

"Chief wants to talk to you. He'll let you know what you have to do."

They followed him down the hall to Olen's office. Olen was filing papers into a folder on his desk when his guests arrived. He stood up to shake Richard's hand and to say hello to Candy. Cooper left the room leaving the couple and Sean to sort things out with the Chief.

Olen looked at Sean when he spoke.

"Am I going to have to lock you up again to keep you out of trouble?"

Sean looked at his father and mother before answering.

"No, sir. Trouble does seem to be finding me a lot here lately but I'm not looking for it. Today was a mistake on my part. I shouldn't have let myself been drawn into a fight. But I can't say someone else might not want to take a swing at me. Bobby and I appear to have already been tried and convicted."

"Sean does have a point, Chief Brown. He has tried to stay at home but he can't hide forever. People are ready to believe the worst of him before even knowing the facts." Candy wanted Olen to see that Sean wasn't to blame in this.

"I can understand that, ma'am. At the same time, I can't set an officer to follow your son everywhere he goes just to keep people from starting trouble with him. He needs to stay low until we can get this thing solved."

"I'll follow him if I need to." Richard didn't know how he was going to do that and work but he felt like Sean needed him more right now than his job did. He had some vacation time saved up, he could afford to take a couple of weeks off.

Olen sighed, running his fingers through his hair. If he didn't believe in his heart that this boy was innocent, he would already have him sitting in a cell. But, the lady that worked at the store told the deputies that the other two boys had started the fight. He was waiting on their parents to pick them up, too.

"Alright, Sean, listen up. I'm going to let you go home one more time. I don't want to see you back in here again, understand?"

"Yes, sir. I'll stay at home if I have to. I'm sorry I've been causing you trouble. I'm not what people think I am. Bobby was right. It's time we grew up." He looked at Richard when he said the last. Richard was torn between applause that his son was showing some responsibility and sadness that these boys wouldn't be allowed to be children just a little while longer.

"ok Take your son home. Keep him out of trouble, please."

"We will. And thank you. Sean could be in a lot worse shape than he is in and I think he knows it. We all know it. If there is any new information on the investigation will you let us know?"

"Sure. Thanks for coming in." Olen stood back up until they had all left his office. Before he could get comfortable though, another set of parents were shown into his office.

Chapter 9

The bleachers were empty except for the lone man watching the practice. His eyes were on number 9, the quarterback. Number 9 fell back two steps, swung left and deftly tossed the ball to the running back who was wide open. With the ball tucked under his arm, number 13 headed for the goal line. After a few fancy dance moves celebrating the touchdown, number 13 was congratulated by his teammates. The man in the bleachers didn't care. He was only interested in the kid with the number 9 jersey.

Sean Branford walked over to the Gatorade jug on the sidelines. He grabbed a cup and gulped it down. He wasn't aware of the attention he was getting from the bleachers. Doug stepped down onto the football field intent on his prey. He still wasn't sure what he wanted to say to this boy but it would come to him.

Sean looked up as Doug came near.

"Are you Sean Branford?"

"Yeah. Who are you?"

"I'm Detective Doug Shankles from the Hot Spring County Sheriff's Office. I'd like to talk to you."

"Uh, I'm kind of busy. What do you want to talk to me for?"

"I have some questions to ask you about a girl named Kimberly Short. Did you know her?" Doug watched Sean's face to gauge his response when he said Kim's name. He saw the recognition and also the trace of fear.

"Yeah, I knew her. I mean she went to school here so everyone knows about her."

"How well did you know her?"

"I don't know, I knew her pretty well, I guess. I had some classes with her."

Coach Edwards walked over to them, interrupting the conversation.

"Hello. Can I help you with something?"

"Hi. I'm Deputy Doug Shankles from the Hot Spring County Sheriff's Office. I'm just asking Sean here some questions about an investigation we have going on right now."

"What does Sean have to do with any investigation? He hasn't had time to get into trouble. We've had practice just about every day. This boy is going to lead us to State next year."

"Really? Well I won't keep him long, then, I just need a little information. Do you mind if he talks to me for a few minutes?"

"I don't guess so. I'll tell the other boys to take a break. Sean, you tell him what he wants to know, ok? We need to get back to practice."

"Sure thing, Coach. What were you asking me about Kim for?"

"I was asking how well you knew Kim. Did you ever date her?"

"No. I didn't know her that well."

Doug could smell the lie from five feet away. He wasn't going to let him off that easy.

"Let's go sit over here and talk, shall we?"

Doug led the way to the bleachers where he had sat just moments ago. Sitting down, he turned back to Sean who had sat down a few feet away. Doug smiled. If Sean thought a little distance was going to help him, he was quite mistaken.

"Well, Sean, it's like this. I know for a fact that you did date Kim. In fact, you were dating her right before she died. Do you want to change your story before we go any farther?"

Sean sank a little lower on the bleacher seat. If he could sink through it, he probably would have. Doug could see the indecision on his face. Should he stick to his story and hope Doug was bluffing or come clean now?

"Yes, sir. I dated her. She wasn't suppose to tell anybody, though. She didn't want people thinking she was dating me just because I'm the quarterback."

"Did you two ever get intimate?"

Sean shifted on the bench. "No. She wouldn't let me get close to her."

Doug waited a minute before asking the next question.

"Knowing Kim as you did, wouldn't you say writing was important to her? And knowing that, wouldn't you assume that she would keep a diary? Most young girls do and it's amazing how much they will say in a diary that they wouldn't say to anyone else."

That got his attention. The air went out of Sean. He knew he was caught like a fly in a spider's web.

"I don't know what she wrote down but I'm telling the truth. I think I need to get back to practice now."

Doug watched Sean get up and start inching back to the football field. He wanted to leave the boy with one more thing to think about before he let him go.

"ok But remember this, DNA results don't lie, people do. And I think we have all the DNA evidence we need to see who's telling the truth. Hope your practice goes well."

Doug got up slowly and casually walked away. He could feel the looks he was getting from the boy behind him. He wondered how long it would take him before he figured out he was truly caught.

....

Mike was having a ball. Malone was like a hornet whose nest had just been hit with a stick. All it took was a little side remark to Olen about the "simmering looks and heat coming off" of Malone and Evangeline, and Malone was threatening to hang Mike by his nether parts.

Olen tried to bring things back to the investigation and keep Malone from strangling Mike.

"Everything Evangeline has told us fits the scene. I don't care how she knows it at this point. If she can help us solve this murder, she'll have my eternal gratitude."

"Chief, I don't know how she does it either. If she is telling the truth about her visions, which I believe she is, this may be a burden on her but a blessing for us." Mike couldn't imagine what it would be like to have that kind of a dream and wake up knowing it had really happened.

"Malone, what do you make of the information? Do you have any clue as to who might have done this?"

"I've been thinking about that. Evangeline said the man was disappointed in her for being pregnant. He felt glad she was dead. That points to the boyfriend. But knowing teenage boys, they would be too stupid to pull this off. Boys are sloppy, he would have left clues, made mistakes. This murder was too clean. This killer knew what he was doing."

Olen was thinking of his own daughter when he said, "So who else does that give us? The father? I know if my teenage daughter came home and told me she was pregnant, I would be mighty disappointed. Of course, I wouldn't kill her over it either."

"I saw the look on her dad's face when I told him she was pregnant. There was genuine shock on his face. I don't think he knew about it before we told him." Mike was remembering the interview with the Shorts.

"Well, then let's go with the boyfriend. Have we had any luck in proving it was Sean Fisher?"

Mike answered, "He denies he knew her. Of course if we could speed up the DNA results that might make it a little easier."

Malone rubbed his day-old growth of beard. "What about blood type? We could get that pretty quick and it could either rule him out or tighten up the case against him."

"That's a good idea. Malone, you think you could run down to the coroner's office and see if he could give us that? I don't remember seeing it in the preliminary report." Olen went to get the file the coroner had sent over after the autopsy.

"Yeah, Malone, why don't you go get that for us. You might want to stop off at Evangeline's before you go. She might want to ride around with you and steam up the windows in your car." Mike couldn't resist one more little jab now that the old Malone was back.

"If you don't shut up, I'll be using you to wipe my windows." Malone's statement was backed up with a snarl.

Olen came back with the file. "No, blood type isn't listed. We need to see if we can get that information. What else did she say? She said the killer left his car near the scene and that it was a red Toyota. What about DMV records. I know there is bound to be a lot of red Toyota's in the state but it's a start. We can look at the list of people who drive red Toyota's and cross reference them with who knew Kim personally."

Mike spoke up, "I can get that for us. I'll try to narrow down the list to only those good possibilities."

"Great. Anybody know if Doug made it back from the prosecutors yet?"

"I haven't seen him, but then again I've been in here with you two. If I see him on my way out, you want me to tell him you're looking for him?" Malone was itching to get going. Now that they had something to go on, he could feel his adrenaline start pumping.

"Yeah, Mike and I will start looking for red Toyota's."

The three separated, each intent on their own tasks to accomplish. Evangeline had re-started the investigation for them. If they had only known, one of them was about to uncover a wolf.

. . . .

Jim Short headed into his office at precisely 8 o'clock. His secretary smiled and said good morning but she wasn't expecting a reply. Everyone in the office knew Jim still wasn't ready to talk about Kim's death so they let him have his space.

Jim's desk was cluttered with paperwork, insurance quotes, letters from attorneys, and repair bills waiting for his approval. He had always taken pride in his job as an insurance adjuster. His desk never had more than a couple of items waiting for him to take care of. Now, he didn't even want to look at it all. He couldn't help but wonder how long it would be before he could start to live again.

He sat in his chair looking at the picture of Kim on his desk. It was taken at an awards ceremony the previous year for outstanding achievements in journalism. Her smile told of how much the award had meant to her. Jim and Rebecca were so proud of her. It wasn't fair that someone so happy and talented had been taken from them. Jim wished he could go back in time and hold her one more time.

The desk calendar with his appointments went unnoticed while Jim reflected on the questions he still had about his daughters death. He wondered how the police were coming on finding whoever had done this. Maybe if they found out who and why someone had killed his little girl, he and Rebecca could finally begin to heal.

. . . .

Doug headed into the office, excited about the information he had for Olen. Not finding him in his office, Doug went in search of him. He nearly collided with Mike coming around the corner.

"There you are, Doug. Chief's been looking for you all day. Where you been hiding at?"

"I've been trying to solve this case, since no one else around here seems to be doing it." Doug's smile took away any real meaning behind his words.

"Ha. Ha. While you've been out gallivanting, we've been here slaving away running down leads."

"Well, let's see if what I have and what you have can piece together some more of the puzzle."

The two walked back to Mike's office to find Olen staring at a computer screen.

"Chief, Doug's back. He seems to think we've been twiddling our thumbs while he's been doing all the work."

Olen replied, "What did you find out at the Prosecutor's office?"

"Nothing good. He's hell bent on charging Bobby and Sean no matter what. We could walk in there with a signed confession and the killer with blood still on his hands and it wouldn't do any good. He seems to believe we need to get out and find him some more evidence, no matter how we get it."

Olen frowned. "That sounds about like Steve. I don't like deadlines, guys, but it looks like we've got one. I've seen what he can do in a courtroom in front of a jury. If we don't solve this, those boys don't stand a chance."

Mike looked at Doug. "I thought you said you were out solving the case? What did you dig up?"

"Well, not much really. I just found the boyfriend is all." Doug's smug look made Mike start to laugh.

"Alright, fill us in, would you?"

Doug told them both about his morning interviews and his trip to the High School stadium. He finished by saying they could probably be expecting a call or a visit from one scared quarterback.

Olen spoke first. "Good. I'd like to talk to this young man. Do you think he's good for this murder or just a jerk of a boyfriend?"

"I don't know for sure but I'm guessing the latter. He doesn't strike me as the violent type. He'd probably have no problem with just dumping the poor girl and picking up the next conquest on his list."

"Chief, do you think we could get a warrant for his DNA so we can match him up as the father of Kim's baby?" Mike asked.

"I don't know. The judge might have a hard time giving us that one since we don't have any real evidence linking him to her. Hearsay and a diary aren't enough for him to issue a warrant on. Maybe we should try talking Sean in to giving us one. You talked to him Doug, do you think we could get it?"

"It might be worth a try. If we bring him in, we might could scare him in to offering us one. If he really does have a career in football, he will want to protect it from a public investigation." Either way, Doug wanted to talk to Sean again to see if he would change his story.

"Why don't you see if you can get a phone number for him and give him a call? Just ask if he would be willing to come in and talk to us."

Olen wanted to see if talking in an interrogation room would make a difference in the young man's story.

"I'll go see what I can do. What are you guys working on?" Doug looked at the computer screen Olen had been working on minutes before.

"Evangeline came in this morning with some more information. The killer was driving a red Toyota according to her vision. We've been trying to search DMV records for anyone connected to Kim who drives a red Toyota." Mike filled Doug in on the rest of Evangeline's visit including the response from Malone.

"I don't know about taking information from her as the gospel. How do we know she is really seeing the truth and not just having a dream?" Doug still wasn't totally convinced Evangeline was the answer to solving this case.

"She just knows too much about the crime itself. Stuff no one has been told and only someone who was there or has seen it would know." Olen was just going on instinct that Evangeline wasn't involved in the murder.

"Have you found anything yet on the records?"

"We've found several red Toyotas locally but none of the names stand out yet. We're still digging. Mike's looking at those in surrounding counties. Nothing we have says this guy is from around here."

"Alright, I'll let you two get back to looking. I'm going to talk to a couple of parents about football season."

Doug left out leaving Mike and Olen free to get back to their computers. Every now and then, Mike stopped to look at the picture on his desk of Amanda. Any thoughts of giving up flew out of his head. Someone's little girl was expecting him to solve this case. Mike would be damned before he let her down.

. . . .

Malone got the blood type from the coroners office. As he was heading back to the station, he passed by Rosa's Floral and Gift Shop. On a whim, he pulled in and parked. Going through the doors, he felt awkward as the lady at the desk asked if he needed any help. Malone stopped in front of a bouquet of lilies and baby's breath. As he asked the lady to package them up, he could see again a picture of a smiling face on a swing. He wondered what it would take to bring that smile back.

. . . .

In a small, dimly lit room across town, a man sat staring at a piece of paper. The words repeating themselves down the page seemed to vibrate through his mind. Even now he believed he had done the right thing. He had to do it. She had forced his hand and there was no going back. The paper proved she knew what had to be done.

So why was he sitting here questioning it now? People needed him. Getting up from his chair, he placed the folded sheet of paper in the big black book sitting on his table. No one would look there. His secret was safe for now. For now, life could move on. He knew he should probably get rid of the paper but he couldn't bring himself to destroy it. When the voice began to question his reasoning, he could pull it out as proof that he had been right. Turning off the small lamp, he took his keys from the table and went to the parked red Toyota sitting in the drive.

....

Linda Timmons shut off the Buick and sat staring at the steering wheel. All her anger had dissipated on the drive home from the beauty shop, leaving only sadness to take it's place. Looking at the front door of her small, three bedroom home, she tried to work up the nerve to go in and face her kids.

Carrying the small bag of groceries, she opened the door and was greeted with the smell of spaghetti sauce and garlic bread. Bobby peeked around the corner of the kitchen with an oven mitt on his hand.

"Hi, Mom. Supper's almost ready. Do you need help with the groceries?"

"No, thanks, I've got them."

Linda set the bag on the counter watching Bobby as he took the bread from the oven and set it on the stove. Jamie wasn't in the kitchen but music was coming from her room so Linda knew where she was. Jamie had spent a lot of time in her room lately listening to the latest teen pop star, Hailey something-or-other.

"Bobby, come sit down for a minute. I want to talk to you."

Linda knew that putting it off wouldn't make it any easier to tell. Bobby could tell something was really wrong so he sat in the chair closest to his mom.

"What is it, Mom? What's wrong?"

"I got fired today from my job. Well, not fired, actually, just asked nicely to pack up my supplies and find another shop to work at."

Bobby sat stunned for a moment, finally looking down at his shoes.

"It's because of me, isn't it? I'm the reason they ask you to leave."

Linda saw the hurt on his face even as he sat staring at the floor. She noticed he was scuffing the heel of his shoe on the linoleum, the same way he had when she told him his father had left them. She walked over and dropped down on her knees in front of him. She took his face in her hands and lifted it so he could see her.

"Look at me, Bobby. This is not your fault. People sometimes can't see the truth even if it jumped up and bit them on the nose. Barbara said she just couldn't handle the publicity she was getting from me being there. A lot of our regular clients have found other shops to go to and the new ones we are getting are thrill seekers just wanting to hear the gory details. We'll be alright. Don't you worry about a thing. The police will find out who killed that poor girl and you and Sean will be cleared. You wait and see."

"How can you be sure? What if they don't find anyone else? You said it yourself, everyone in town believes we did it so a trial would be a joke. Sometimes I get so angry but I don't know who with. Should I be angry at God for letting this happen or just be angry with myself for being so stupid?"

"You're not stupid Bobby. What you and Sean did wasn't a crime. It was just teenage boys being just that. God won't let you and Sean pay for this crime. You both will be cleared, I'll get another job and life will go on."

Bobby looked at his mother and saw the faith in her eyes. She had been through so much and still she was strong. Guilt for his part in her hardships made him vow to do whatever it took to make her life easier from now on.

Linda stood up, grabbed his hands and said, "Come on, call your sister and let's eat some of your famous spaghetti with meatballs."

....

Sean Fisher was at that moment sitting on a four wheeler looking over the mountain view near his home. His father, sitting on his four wheeler, turned from the view of the mountain to look at his son. Sean had changed in the past few weeks, understandably so. Yet Richard couldn't help but wish a little piece of the laughing, carefree Sean would resurface soon.

"It's beautiful, isn't it Dad?"

"Yep. Peaceful, too. Sometimes I think I must have been a mountain man in a previous life. I could get lost up here and never miss a thing from the real world. Well, maybe your Mom, but then again…"

Sean laughed. "I'm sure she'd miss you, too." He paused for a moment and then, "Can I ask you something?"

"Sure."

"What made you and Mom choose me? I mean, there must have been a lot of babies to choose from. What made you want me?"

Richard could sense the need in Sean, the need to know you are loved for who you are. He looked back into the past and saw again that red headed infant looking up at him and knew his answer.

"Love. Your Mom could tell from the time she looked into your eyes that you belonged to us. I tried to act like it was her decision but I knew it, too. I can't explain it very well but it was just a gut feeling, I guess. We didn't have to look any farther, it was if you truly were born to us. We still love you, more today than seventeen years ago."

"Don't you wish sometimes that you had picked another kid? Maybe one who didn't cause so much trouble?" Sean looked at his father, almost holding his breath.

"Not for one second. Trouble just seems to make you realize how much you need those you love the most. Don't get the wrong idea, I wish this wasn't happening to us but we can get through it. Your Mom might be smothering you right now but that's her way of dealing with it. She's the type that always has to be fixing things, whether it be the housework or people. It's just her way."

" I know. It doesn't bother me. I want you to know how sorry I am for all this. If I could go back and change it I would."

"I know you would. But don't let this change you too much, Sean. Don't lose yourself somewhere along the line. You've got to have laughter in your life. I'd like to see more of that again."

Sean looked at the man who had always been there for him when he needed him. Richard may not have been as affectionate as Candy had but Sean had always known he loved him. Now, he wanted to get on with his life, start over a little.

"I'll race you to the bottom."

"You're on, son. But don't come crying to me when all you see is dust in your eyes."

The sound of the ATV's roaring into life cut across the stillness of the mountain. Father and son chased the wind, laughter floating back to the trees and to the ghosts of the mountain men who came before them.

Chapter 10

Sean Branford walked into the Sheriff's Office with his father at 10:00 the next morning. The future star quarterback didn't look as sure of himself in this setting as he did on the football field. Doug met them at the front desk and led them back to Interrogation Room 1. Once they were settled in their chairs, Doug asked if either wanted water or a soft drink. Both refused.

"ok let's get right down to why we are here."

"I didn't get my boy a lawyer, do I need to?" Brian Branford wasn't sure what to expect. After the phone call he had received last night, his world had turned topsy-turvy.

Doug assured him, "No, sir, Sean is not under arrest at this time. We just have a few questions to ask him. This is completely voluntary. You are both free to leave at any time."

"Sean says you already talked to him yesterday, what else do you need to know?"

"Well, we need to clarify some of his answers. I would like to record this interview for our records, if that is alright with you."

"That's fine with us. We don't have anything to hide."

Doug began, "Sean, you said you had dated Kimberly but that you had not had sex, is that correct?"

"Yeah, that's what I said." Sean wouldn't look at Doug when he answered.

"Would you like to change that answer before we go any further?"

Sean looked over at his father.

"Don't look at me, boy, just answer the man truthfully. Did you have sex with the girl or not?"

"Yes, sir, I did."

"Then why'd you go and lie to the man yesterday when he asked you that?"

"I was scared. Scared I'd get in trouble, I guess."

"Well, it looks like you're in a heap more trouble now," his father replied.

Doug stepped in. "Sean, did Kim tell you she was pregnant?"

"Yes sir, she did."

Brian broke in, "Pregnant? Boy, why didn't you tell us about this?"

"Because I didn't want to ruin my chances at football. I thought if you knew, you might make me quit football to work or something."

"Damn right you would have worked. But you wouldn't have had to give up football. That's your dream, son. What did you tell this girl when she told you she was pregnant?"

"I told her I didn't want it, the baby, I mean. I told her not to call me anymore, that the baby probably wasn't mine anyways."

Brian came out of his chair at that. Startled, Doug stood up and was ready to come between them if need be. Brian didn't attempt to hit him but Sean flinched all the same.

"How could you, boy? How could you tell that poor girl something so stupid? How long had you been seeing her?"

"About 7 months."

"Did she date anyone else? Was she the type to sleep around?"

Sean wasn't even attempting to look up at his father anymore. His eyes stayed trained on the speck of dried coffee stain on the floor.

"No, she hadn't dated anyone before me that I know of. She hadn't slept around either. I was her first."

"You mean she was a virgin and you go and tell her the baby probably wasn't yours? I thought I had raised you better than that, son."

Doug sat back down. "Sean, you know this doesn't look good. You admit that you were dating her and that she had just told you she was pregnant. Doesn't it seem more than a coincidence that she turns up dead a few days later?"

Sean looked up then. He looked directly at Doug and said, "I couldn't have done it. I was at football practice that morning. You can ask anybody on the team, coach can tell you too."

"That's true, Deputy. I took him to practice myself that day." Brian had returned to his seat.

"Then that should be easy to verify. I appreciate you telling the truth, Sean. Don't you think Kim deserves that much?"

"Yes, sir. Can I go home now?"

"Yes, you can go."

As the three were walking to the door, Sean turned around and seemed to gather the nerve to ask, "Could they tell what it was? The baby, was it a boy or a girl?"

Doug was surprised at his question. He hadn't expected Sean to care about the child he had denied. All the same, he answered.

"A boy. It was a little boy."

Sean dropped his head down to his chest as he walked from the room. Doug watched him leave hoping that this would leave an imprint of change on the young man's heart.

....

With their first appearance in court looming, both Sean and Bobby's families were in a state of confusion. On one hand, they were all ready for this to be over and done with. Yet no one had a clue as to how it would turn out. Sean's lawyer assured his parents that the state's case against him was completely circumstantial. No solid evidence linked either of the boys to the crime. But anxiety still reigned.

The first court appearance was merely a formality really. They were to come before the judge to enter their pleas. Both were pleading not guilty. The prosecutor made an appointment with Bobby's attorney first. If there was a weakness, Bobby would be the one. A court appointed attorney was usually willing to plead his client out, whether he thought he was innocent or not. With a heavy case load and little pay or recognition, it just wasn't worth their time to go to a jury.

Samuel Franks was no exception. He walked into Steve's office, plopped down in the chair, and set his briefcase on the floor. Samuel was a short man, with balding grey hair, a thin mustache and a disheveled appearance. His brown business suit looked as if he had slept in it for a couple of days before making his way to the office. At one time, straight out of law school, he had cared about his appearance. Wearing crisp, clean suits with bold colored ties, he strutted into a court room as if he owned it. Years of plea agreements, dishonest judges with payouts in their pockets, and prosecutors with hidden agendas, had taught Samuel that you won't get rich by doing the right thing and nobody even cared if you did.

Looking at him now, Steve wondered how the man managed to keep track of his clients. It didn't even appear as if he could dress himself properly much less aggressively represent anyone. Still, he smiled at the man in front of him.

"Good to see you, Samuel. Glad you could come over so quick."

"Wasn't doing much else today. All my trials aren't set to start until next week."

"Good, good. Let's get right down to the heart of the matter. How about I take one of those cases off your hands. You know Bobby Timmons was found beside the body of the victim in this case. He had her blood on his hands and clothing. The jury isn't going to buy his innocence story."

"But you don't have a murder weapon. If he was sitting right beside her, what did he do with the knife, swallow it?"

"That's a minor detail. I could make it plausible that there was a third boy involved who took the knife and was getting rid of it for them when the boys were discovered. I don't think the jury would have any doubt that's what happened. These boys are skating on thin ice. By the time I get done painting the picture of a poor, innocent 16 year old girl who had her whole life ahead of her, these boys will be lucky to get life without parole."

"What are you offering?"

"Plead to negligent homicide, 15 years, maybe 12 with good behavior, and they'll be out in time to get married and have a houseful of kids."

"Ten with 5 years probation."

"You know I can't do that. The whole town would be after my hide. We've got to at least make it look like they're paying for the crime."

"I'll have to get with my client. I'm not sure he'll go for it. He seems pretty set on proving he's innocent."

"Make him want to go for it. Just think, one less case for you, the taxpayers are happy, and justice is served. Maybe you'd even have time for a vacation."

"I'll have you an answer by tomorrow."

Samuel got up to leave. He made it to the door before he realized he had forgotten his briefcase beside the chair. After he left, Steve smiled to himself. Life was good. Re-election was coming up, his conviction rate was up, and he could tell the fine citizens that they could rest easy at last. Steve wasn't use to not getting what he wanted. It never occurred to him that it might not be as easy as it seemed.

···........

Cooper strolled into the Sheriff's office with a double mocha latte from the local coffee shop in his hands. As he walked past the secretary's office, he noticed her leaning over the copy machine putting in more copy paper. Grinning to himself, he tiptoed up behind her, slapped her on the behind and stepped out of her way when she swung around with a jerk. Marsha clutched the crumpled paper to her chest as she glared at Cooper.

Cooper started laughing as Marsha stomped off to her desk. Muttering to herself, she shot daggers at him as he walked back down the hall. God, she hated that man. She couldn't understand why the Chief kept him on. Who cares if he's the Sheriff's nephew? They needed to get rid of him. Either that or someone was going to shoot him. Marsha doubted anyone would miss him.

Cooper made his way to Olen's office just as Olen was leaving. When he saw Cooper, he sighed, not looking forward to the conversation he was about to have. Postponing it wouldn't help though. Better to have it out now.

"Cooper, you were suppose to be here an hour ago. Where have you been?"

"Sorry, Chief. I got caught in a traffic jam." Cooper said with a lopsided smile.

"Have you forgotten where we are? I have a scanner in my office and there hasn't been a traffic jam all day. Come on in and sit down. We need to talk."

Cooper followed Olen into the office and sat down while Olen closed the door. Cooper never seemed to be concerned about anything. That insincere smile was ever present on his face. Olen wasn't fooled for a minute. He had finally figured out what made Cooper tick.

"Mark, you've been with this department for three years now. In that time I've had ten interdepartmental complaints on you and fifteen citizen complaints. Look at your folder. We could use it for a stepping stool."

Olen slapped the folder on his desk, making the pen cup rattle. Cooper didn't seem too concerned.

"What can I say? I'm popular."

"This is serious, Mark. The only reason you are still here and not cleaning toilets down the hall is because of your uncle."

Cooper's smile faltered a bit. For Olen to be admitting that, it must be serious.

"Don't let that stop you. If you got a problem with me, let's hear it."

"I've been thinking about you and it puzzles me why you would deliberately do the things you do, knowing that it could lead to a dismissal. So I've come to the conclusion that you want to be fired. That in turn leads me to think you're not happy."

Mark slid his gaze away from Olen's. The smile was gone now, replaced instead with a furrowed brow. He looked out the window, absently watching as the next shift got into their cars and headed out on duty. No one had ever taken the time to notice him. At least not unless he was in trouble.

Olen continued, "What do you want to do with your life, Mark? Do you want to spend it here, in this department? If so, your behavior can't continue. I can't keep protecting you."

Mark finally looked back at Olen before speaking again.

"What do you want me to say? Everyone has always told me what to do, when to do it, and how to do it. I've never had a choice in my career. It was expected of me to be a cop so I became a cop. Too late to change it now."

Olen suspected as much. "Do you want to change it is the question I am asking you?"

"What else is there? I'm not qualified to do anything else. All my training has been in police work. I ain't exactly scholarly, if you know what I mean."

Olen sat back in his chair, crossing his legs. With his fingers steepled under his chin, he watched Mark for a moment. Finally he sat forward, resting his elbows on the desk.

"Mark, you're about to let everyone down."

Olen laid out his plan and waited for a response. It wasn't long before the smile was back. Only this time, it was the genuine article.

....

Driving back to town, Malone was still thinking about something Evangeline had said. At the time he hadn't thought much about it. He had been too pleased with the effect the flowers had had on her. Still, a little voice kept telling him she may have been on to something without even knowing it.

They had been sitting on the couch drinking iced tea. She was talking about the lilies and how it was a shame that most people believed in giving lilies only at funerals. They should be given to people while they are still alive to truly enjoy them.

Thinking back on it, every funeral Malone had ever been too, he had seen lilies. But he couldn't remember seeing any lilies at the funeral home during Kim's funeral. However, he did recall seeing one white lily placed on the casket at the grave sight. It seemed very odd that no one would have sent them to the family. There had been other flowers, potted plants and wreaths, but no lilies. He didn't know what to make of this but he couldn't help but think it was important for him to find out. Maybe it was nothing but he decided to go with his gut instinct. First stop would be the funeral home.

Chapter 11

The funeral director was a little intimidated by the big man standing in front of him asking him about flowers. He wasn't used to people questioning the arrangements in his funeral home. His professionalism had earned The Regency Funeral Home a sterling reputation in the small community.

Smiling up at the Officer, he admitted that he remembered that funeral very clearly. The situation being as it was, he personally had overseen all the arrangements. The local floral shops had sent over multitudes of floral arrangements with lilies. However, due to the family's request, all those containing lilies had been sent back to be replaced with other flowers.

Malone frowned. Why did the family request that no lilies be sent, he asked? The Director did not know, he only knew that the Reverend Peterson had passed on the request. Perhaps the Detective could ask the Reverend.

Malone thanked the man and left the funeral home. Getting into his car, he realized that he now had more questions than before he had went in. His next stop would be talking to a preacher.

....

Bobby sat listening to the lawyer the court had assigned him. Looking at the crumpled piece of a man, Bobby didn't have a lot of hope that his trial would turn out like he wanted it to. Especially if what he was saying now was any indication of what he could expect.

"Let me get this straight." Bobby said. "You want me to not only say I did it, which I didn't, but to also agree to go to jail for 15 years? Are you nuts?"

"Young man, you don't understand the legal system like I do. I'm trying to help you. If you don't accept a plea agreement, you're looking at life without parole or maybe even the death penalty, depending on what kind of a jury you get. If you plead guilty, you would get 15 years and be out in 10 with good behavior. You'd still have your whole life ahead of you."

"I also have a chance at proving I'm innocent. They have nothing to prove I did it. No weapon, no motive, no nothing. How can a jury possibly find me guilty?" Bobby couldn't understand why everyone still thought he was a murderer.

"It doesn't matter. The prosecutor is good at his job. He can prove you were at the scene and you had that young girls blood on you. The jury will put the rest together all by themselves. How can you prove you didn't do it?"

"That's what you're suppose to do. Isn't that what you get paid for?"

Samuel bristled up at his tone. He didn't like a seventeen year old trying to tell him how to do his job.

"I wouldn't be doing my job properly if I didn't get you an offer like this. The prosecutor was hard enough to convince to give you this lenient of a sentence. He wanted to go for twenty but I got him down. I think it would be in your best interests to consider it. If we go to trial, this offer will disappear."

"Well I think I'll take my chances, thank you. I won't lie and say I killed her. If I go to prison, at least I go knowing I am innocent."

Samuel stood up, glancing around the small living room of Bobby's home. Everywhere he looked, he saw evidence of a loving family. Pictures of the kids or Linda, laughing into the camera, lined the walls. Samuel wondered how this boy was going to handle being torn away from all this? For a moment, a glint of the old Samuel was back, wanting to fight for the innocent. Yet as he turned, his eyes shuttered, he realized the fight just wasn't in him anymore.

"Think about what I said. Talk to your mom about it and give me a call. I can have this all settled within a week."

"I don't want a week, I want a lifetime. Free and clear. I want people to look at me again without glancing away quickly wondering what kind of a boy would do that to another human being. Can you wrap that up in a week?"

Samuel didn't reply. He walked to the front door and let himself out. Bobby watched him drive away before falling back to the couch. Putting his face in his hands, Bobby did the only thing he knew to do anymore. He prayed.

....

Malone called the office to get the address of Reverend Peterson. He talked to Mike and told him his findings so far. Mike agreed with Malone, always go with your hunches. Mike hung up after giving him the address and went to find Olen. He couldn't help but feel they were finally getting somewhere. He also wanted to go back over the DMV records. He had his own gut instincts to follow.

....

Reverend Peterson answered his door to find a burly man standing on his step. He didn't want to appear startled so he tried a smile instead.

"Yes, may I help you?", he asked politely.

"You're Reverend Peterson, correct?", Malone asked.

"Yes, I am. And you are?"

"I'm Detective Malone with the Hot Spring County Sheriffs Department. I need to ask you a few questions about Kimberly Short. Can I come in?"

The Reverend stepped aside.

"Yes, come into the living room. I was just working on my sermon for Sunday but it can wait. I am always here to help when I can."

Reverend Peterson led the way to the roomy living area, moving his Bible and papers off of the couch so Malone could have a seat. Malone took a look around before sitting down on the sofa. The home seemed nice and neat, something Malone pictured a preacher having. Crosses lined the walls along with black and white pictures of a man in a Navy uniform and a woman holding a small child in her arms.

Malone was curious about the man. It wasn't just the questions he had about this case. He had always wondered what made a person want to devote his life to preaching to people who most of the time were only there to impress others. Malone had never been a religious man although there had been times during the war that all you could do was pray.

Reverend Peterson sat looking at the Detective, wondering what he was thinking about his home. Finally, clearing his throat, he spoke.

"You said you had some questions about Kimberly Short. Such a sad waste, her death. She was a bright, young girl, full of life. I believe, had she lived, she would have been a real blessing to the church."

Malone was a good judge of character. He could see the ease the man tried to portray. Yet he was nervous, too. Malone wasn't sure if that was due to guilt or just because he had the ability to scare most people out of their wits.

"How well did you know Kim and her family?"

"I've known Jim and Rebecca Short since they moved here in '96. Kim was only about 5 years old at the time I believe. A beautiful family, God fearing, always donating to the church.

In the aftermath of the tornado in '97, Jim and Rebecca opened their home to a local family who had lost everything."

"So they were admired then, you would say?"

"Oh, yes. Everyone loves them. It was a great shock to hear of Kim's murder."

"What about the funeral arrangements? Did the Shorts handle that themselves or did they leave that to you?" Malone watched for any signs of falsehood. The eyes were a better lie detector than any machine could ever be.

"If I remember correctly, Rebecca's sister handled most of the arrangements. I was told how they wanted the service to be, but most everything else was handled by the family."

"What about the flowers? Did the family have a preference on the floral arrangements?" Malone could see a shift in the man's gaze. Just a flinch, really.

"I don't think so. Most families don't concern themselves with such mundane things at a time like that."

"I was told by the funeral director, a Mr. Roberts, that you sent back some of the floral arrangements that contained lilies, based on a family request."

"Well, yes, in a way."

"What way is that? Did the family ask for no lilies?"

"Not in exact words. They told me they wanted the funeral to be a tribute to Kim, a true picture of Kim's life. I felt lilies would have been inappropriate." The Reverend got up and moved to a nearby table. He ran his fingers over his worn Bible. Malone watched his movements for a moment before asking,

"Why would that be, Reverend?"

"Detective, do you know what the lily symbolizes? Innocence, purity. The lily is the flower most people associate with funerals. The lily symbolizes that the soul of the departed has received restored innocence after death. Of course the white lily symbolizes purity and chastity as it is associated with the Virgin Mary. That is why I didn't feel that lilies should be present at Kim's funeral. It would have painted a false picture of purity and innocence. "

"What do you mean? Kim was a young, teenage girl. I would think she would be the perfect picture of innocence."

"It would have been, I suppose. Only I was saddened to learn that Kim had allowed herself to be seduced by a young man at school. It seems she was with child at the time of her death. Surely your investigation would have shown this?"

"Yes, actually we did find that out thanks to the autopsy. However, no one else was aware of the fact, that we knew of. How did you come by such information, Reverend?"

"I don't recall, actually. Perhaps the family informed me of the fact."

Malone's internal radar was going berserk. If superstition were to be believed, either lightening was going to strike the good Reverend or a fire was about to erupt in his nether regions. Either way, Malone was going to be several feet away just to be on the safe side.

"But, Reverend, I recall a single, white lily being placed on Kim's casket before it was lowered. How did it get there?"

The Reverend actually looked angry for a moment, indecision and guilt crossing his features. Then he relaxed.

"I placed it there. I felt that in death, Kim had been restored to her innocence and washed clean of her sins." He was still running his fingers over the black cover of his Bible as he spoke. It seemed to calm him.

"What gave you the right to decide Kim's innocence or loss of virtue?" Malone was angry now. He had always hated self-righteous prigs and this one was full of himself.

Reverend Peterson seemed surprised at the anger in Malone's voice.

"Why God gave me that right, Detective. I am his appointed vessel and he uses me to serve his needs. I am to give my flock guidance to live as God commands in this book."

He held up the Bible as he spoke. Continuing, he said,

"I listen to my congregation, to each member and guide him or her to the path of righteousness. Kim strayed from that path but a moment, yet I helped her to regain her footing."

"How did you help, Reverend? By stabbing her to death?"

Malone watched for the response to his accusation. It wasn't long in coming.

"Are you familiar with the Bible, Detective? Do you remember your Bible stories as a child? Genesis chapter 22: 'And he said, Take now thy son, thine only son Isaac, whom thou lovest, and get thee into the land of Moriah; and offer him there for a burnt offering upon one of the mountains which I will tell thee of. And they came to the place which God had told him of; and Abraham built an altar there, and laid the wood in order, and bound Isaac his son, and laid him on the altar upon the wood. And Abraham stretched forth his hand, and took the knife to slay his son.' So you see, Detective, God used Abraham, tested him to see if he would follow his will. God stopped Abraham's hand before he could destroy Isaac, for he would become the line to God's chosen people. It was God's will that Isaac live."

"And Kim, it was God's will that she die?"

"I thought he would stop me, so I hesitated at first and he didn't. It was his will that she die to restore her everlasting soul."

Malone just stared at the man, the madness making him believe his own words. The Reverend was gripping the Bible tightly to his chest now, his breathing harsh as if he had been running. He looked up at Malone with a vacant stare before opening the book in his hands. He pulled a single white page from the inside cover, holding it reverently.

Malone knew in his bones what that paper contained, yet he asked,

"What do you have, Reverend?"

Reverend Peterson looked at the paper before smiling.

"Here is proof, Detective. Proof of what I said. Even Kim, in her own heart knew what had to be done. She was writing this as I came upon her."

He handed the paper to Malone. Malone pulled a handkerchief from his pocket before taking the page. The paper contained two things; the words 'forgive me' written all down the page and small drops of dried blood stains.

Malone was not concerned with his own safety at this point. He knew he was dealing with an unstable mind, yet it never occurred to him that his own life would be in danger. As he was wrapping the paper gently in the cloth, a searing cold pain shot through his back.

....

Mike skidded to a halt in front of Olen's door. The door banged on it's hinges as he slammed it opened without knocking. Olen jumped a couple of inches out of his chair before he realized it was just Mike.

"Good God, Mike, you about gave me a heart attack. What's going on?"

"I got it, Chief, I got it. Malone was right." Mike was shaking a piece of paper at Olen.

"What was Malone right about? Calm down and tell what you've got." Olen walked over to get the paper from Mike.

"Malone went to talk to the Reverend. Something about the flowers weren't right. Anyways, after he left, I went back to the DMV records to see what kind of car Reverend Peterson drives. I didn't remember seeing his name on our list but I thought I'd check it out again anyway." Mike couldn't hardly stand still in all his excitement.

Olen looked at the paper before saying,

"So? This is a red Toyota registered to a Lenore Halcomb. What has that got to do with Reverend Peterson?"

"She happens to be the good Reverend's mother. She married Jeremiah Peterson, had one boy child, Geoffery Peterson, before her husband died in an accident at sea. He was a Naval engineer. Seven years later, she met and married Alfred Halcomb. This husband managed to live until six years ago. The aging Mrs. Halcomb lived with her son up until about six months ago when she suffered a stroke. She is now living in Second Haven nursing home. Her car, a red, 2003 Toyota Camry is still registered in her name. That's why we didn't recognize the name. She would have nothing to do with Kim. But the Reverend does."

Olen was already going to his phone.

"Where's Malone now?" Olen asked.

"He went to talk to the Reverend."

"Get some back up and head over there. I'll get the search warrant on the way. I want that car impounded and the Reverend here to answer some questions."

"Yes, sir."

Mike was gone before Olen connected to the courthouse. He grabbed Doug from his office on the way out. Doug was going to get Cooper but Mike said they didn't have time. They could call him on their way.

As they pulled up to Reverend Peterson's home, a red Toyota came pulling out of the garage. Both men jumped out of the car and ran to stop the Reverend from leaving. Doug managed to get the Reverend out of the car and handcuffed while Mike turned off the Toyota.

"Where's Malone?" Doug asked Mike.

"I don't know. His car is still here." Both men had an eerie feeling. Doug shook the Reverend a little as he pulled him up.

"Where's he at?"

"I don't know what you're talking about. I was just leaving to go to the church to practice my sermon. Why are you dragging me out of my car?"

Mike was already heading inside the house.

Reverend Peterson yelled at him, "You can't go in there!"

Mike opened the door to the house. His pistol drawn, Mike inched forward toward the living room. Coming into the room, he spotted Malone lying face down on the carpet with blood leaking to the floor from the knife wound in his back. Mike dropped to the floor calling to Malone.

"Don't you be dead, dammit. Wake up Malone!" He felt for a pulse and was relieved to feel a faint beat beneath his fingers. Using his radio he called for paramedics. Holding his hand over the wound, Mike kept talking to Malone.

"I know you can hear me you big lug. You know you're too stubborn to die. Who's going to hurl insults at me if you're not around, huh?"

Doug came rushing into the room, stopping cold when he saw Malone on the floor.

"Is he..."

"No, he's alive. At least for now. Where's the Reverend?"

"Cooper's got him in his car. For once I hope he beats the crap out of him before stuffing him in there."

"I might just help him."

Malone moaned a little and started to move.

"Stay still, Ben. Hang on. We got help coming, partner." Mike kept repeating it, "Hold on. Just hold on."

The ambulance arrived and the paramedics took over for Mike. Both Mike and Doug stepped out of the way so the men could do their job. Neither said a lot, just stood waiting.

Finally, Malone was loaded onto a stretcher and taken to the ambulance. Mike asked the driver if Malone was going to be alright.

"We'll do everything we can for him."

Before long, the ambulance was out of sight and the street was taped off. Orange police tape surrounded the street and house. Olen was there questioning first the Reverend in the backseat of Cooper's car and then neighbors who had gathered to watch the scene.

Mike knew he needed to start processing evidence but he wanted more than anything to be at the hospital. Olen told him to go. They could get more officers out there to collect everything. Mike didn't need telling twice.

Chapter 12

The small community was abuzz with the news of the capture of the Reverend Peterson and the attack on Sergeant Malone. News crews were back in residence at the police station, vying for information to air on the nightly news. Carol Watkins was once again sent to the station for a report for the newspaper. Everyone waited for information.

Across town in a cold ICU room, Ben Malone was grumpy. Sitting calmly beside his bed was Evangeline. Mike had just left with a smile on his face, knowing his partner was going to be ok If Malone was griping about the tubes coming out of his arms and his face, Mike knew he would make it. Especially since Evangeline was there to care for him.

Thinking about her, Mike was glad she had been there. He had been pacing the emergency room waiting area when she had come in. She managed to calm him and assure him that Ben would be alright. They sat together until the Doctor had come out to inform them that Malone was out of surgery and in the recovery room. He told them that the knife wound was not a severe one and they expected a full recovery. He would have to stay in ICU for a few days to watch for signs of infection but he should be fine in no time.

Mike and Evangeline thanked the Doctor before heading back to see Ben. At first, Mike was shocked to see the big man laid low. Lying on the small bed, which he seemed to envelope, Malone looked so still. His breathing was even, though, and the nurse reassured them that he was resting well.

Mike went home then to see his family. It had been a trying day and he needed his wife's touch and his little girl's smile to help him unwind. Evangeline stayed at the hospital with Malone. She promised to call Mike if anything came up.

In the days that followed, the true events of that day on the river bank came to light. The search of the Reverend's home led to the recovery of the knife that had been used to kill Kimberly Short and also the attack on Sergeant Malone. The lab would have to positively identify the DNA evidence found on the knife but preliminary tests showed two different blood types on the knife.

Reverend Peterson had been taken to the county lock up, pending formal charges. Hot Spring County Prosecutor Steve Kooley was quoted in the media as saying the citizens of Malvern and the surrounding areas could rest easy with the arrest of the Reverend. His continued support of the Hot Spring County Sheriff's Office had led to some fine police work and the capture of the true culprit. When asked about the two boys who had originally been investigated, he stated that he had always been open to the fact that someone else might have committed the crime.

The two boys were enjoying freedom with their families. Richard and Candy Fisher were celebrating by spending the weekend on a camping trip with Sean. School was set to start in a week and all three were relieved that Sean would be able to finish his senior year at Magnet Cove High School without any stain on his reputation.

Bobby Timmons was also looking forward to his senior year. His summer had taught him many things, but none so important as the value of family. He and Sean were easing back into friendship. Gone were the carefree days of boyhood, replaced by the knowledge that every day was important. Yet, life was not all serious. The two were bound to find some smiles along the way.

Linda Timmons was back at Barb's Beauty Shop. Barb had apologized for letting her go. Linda had considered, only for a moment, not going back out of pride. Looking at her children, though, she knew pride wouldn't pay the bills. She looked forward to seeing her regular customers again and being able to hold her head high.

She was also very proud of her son. When he had told her about Samuel Franks' offer, fear and anger had engulfed her. She hadn't felt that way since her husband had left them. Bobby had not been angry. He had only been more determined to prove his innocence.

Cooper had been let go by the Sheriff's Office. He was being transferred back to the Police Academy. This time as an instructor. Olen and Jeremy figured if the recruits could make it through the academy without strangling Mark, they'd have some mighty fine officers to choose from. Cooper was given a massive going away party by the department. Marsha had led the group in speeding Cooper on his way. No one quite understood her enthusiasm at the party.

....

Jim and Rebecca Short were coming to grips with the loss of their daughter. Jim's job was keeping him busy and Rebecca was volunteering at the elementary school. The couple had finally learned the truth about their daughter's death. Kim had went to the Reverend the day before she died, asking for advice from the man she had always trusted. Little had she known where it would lead.

Before Reverend Peterson could go to trial for the murder of Kimberly Short and the attempted murder of Sergeant Ben

Malone, he was found dead in his cell, hanging by his bed sheet from the bars. A full investigation followed into why he was left alone long enough to commit suicide. No charges were ever filed.

Life was starting over for some and moving on for others. Malone was finally able to come back to work, to the delight of all who worked with him. Mike couldn't quit smiling even when Malone told him he looked like a hyena.

On a sunny afternoon, with a soft breeze blowing across the porch swing, Malone sat with Evangeline looking out over the garden. Paix lay at their feet, content to sleep through the day. Malone had never really gotten up the courage to ask Evangeline about her life. He didn't feel that he had the right. He knew when she was ready to tell him she would. He did have misgivings about one thing, though.

"Evangeline, I have never told you thank you for staying with me when I was in the hospital. I know I don't make a good patient and you must have wanted to hit me sometimes."

"I understood. You are used to being in charge. It is hard for a man like that to accept weakness and the need for assistance."

She looked at him thoughtfully. She knew there was something bothering him. She also knew he would bring it up when he could formulate it in his own mind.

He blurted out, "I lied to get into the army. I was only 16 but I always looked so much older. I wanted to be over there fighting. My Dad knew how much I wanted it so he signed for me saying I was 18. I went to Vietnam within a week."

He stopped for a moment, thinking back to the war and what it had done to him.

"You could never imagine what it was like. I don't want you to imagine either. What I'm trying to get at is my age, Evangeline. Even though I lied and said I was 2 years older than I was, it's just 2 years. That still makes me 58 years old."

Evangeline looked at Malone, at the lines on his face, the worn leather look of him. She reached up to lightly run her fingers across his cheek. A smile formed on her face as she softly answered.

"No, Ben. You are 58 years young."

"But I am old enough to be your father."

She shook her head slowly. "Age does not matter to me. Look around you. The earth is millions of years old, yet look at the beauty that surrounds us. Paix is old for his species yet his favorite pastime is chasing the squirrels and rabbits in the garden. Age is determined in spirit, not years."

Malone was humbled by her words. He never expected to find someone he would be sitting like this with. He never expected anyone like her. He was amazed that he felt it with someone who he still only knew by her first name.

As if guessing his thoughts, Evangeline reached out and took his hands, pulling him to his feet. She led the way into her house to stop in front of the pictures on her wall.

Malone stood still, looking again at the picture that always drew his eye. It was Evangeline on a swing, laughing, with the children playing around her.

"My name is Evangeline Gerard. Those are my children, Ettine, my son, and Emille, my daughter. This was taken on April 13th, 1992, two weeks before my husband killed me."

At Malone's startled look of bewilderment, Evangeline began her story…

Coming Soon
Death Envisioned

Growing up on a sugar plantation in Lafayette Louisiana, Evangeline Gerard knew she was different. Visions of death haunted the young girl. The images crept into her sleep, waking her in cold sweats. Only her mother knew the truth of the dreams. As a Cajun healer, Evangeline's mother was believed by many to be a witch. Evangeline learned quickly that being different could lead to violence. So she kept her secret.

She begins to forget about the visions as she begins a new life away from the memories that haunt her. She marries the man of her dreams and spends her time being a mother and a wife. The years pass in contentment until the one night the visions return. Only this time, it isn't a strangers face she sees. For what wakes Evangeline in the dead of night, is images of her own death at the hands of a madman.

www.ingramcontent.com/pod-product-compliance
Lightning Source LLC
Chambersburg PA
CBHW060638130626
46555CB00002B/853